FADEAWAY

FADEAWAY

MAURA ELLEN STOKES

**YELLOW
JACKET**

YELLOW JACKET
an imprint of Bonnier Publishing USA

251 Park Avenue South, New York, NY 10010
Copyright © 2018 by Maura Ellen Stokes
All rights reserved, including the right of reproduction in whole or in part in any form.
Yellow Jacket is a trademark of Bonnier Publishing USA, and associated colophon is a trademark of Bonnier Publishing USA.
Manufactured in the United States of America BVG 0518
First Edition
10 9 8 7 6 5 4 3 2 1
Library of Congress Cataloging-in-Publication Data is available upon request.
ISBN 978-1-4998-0674-8
yellowjacketbooks.com
bonnierpublishingusa.com

To the memory of
Helen Prendergast Stokes

GONE

I pretended Reagan wasn't there when she opened the door and waltzed into my room. I didn't turn in my chair, and I kept my eyes peeled on the summer reading list stuck over my desk.

She flopped onto my unmade bed.

"Good to see you, too," she said.

I didn't answer.

"What?" asked Reagan.

I didn't move. "No one knocked, so I must be alone."

"Excuse me?"

"Knocking—asking to come in," I said.

"Why would I do that? I practically live here."

She had a point. We had been attached at the hip since we reached for the same bouncy ball in kindergarten.

Reagan looked over my shoulder. "No one reads the freshman reading list, Sam-I-am."

"You haven't started, have you?" I said. "You know it's August, right?"

She shrugged. "Hey, you still have it." She pointed to a picture of our first basketball team pinned next to the reading list. Eight-year-old Reagan stood behind me, hands on my shoulder, wearing the yellow Dribble Queen T-shirt she had won that day.

"Yeah. Mom found it in a drawer last night."

"Cool," she said. "When I used to be taller than you."

"Those days are history." We were exactly the same height.

"I haven't finished growing," she said.

"Neither have I."

Reagan stretched her arms over her head. "Ready to go play while you can still defend me?"

"I was thinking of skipping today," I said. "To catch up on my reading."

Reagan chortled. "Right."

I grinned. "Come on." I picked up my basketball from the floor, and we headed to Grant gym for the afternoon pickup game.

———————————

Within minutes of choosing sides, we were playing full court. Reagan and I always played point for opposite sides. She was a better playmaker, and I was a better shot, but no one except us could tell the difference.

Matt Diggers pulled down a long rebound and threw it to me. We raced to the other end. I looked left to Maddie Smith, but I took on Reagan to go to the basket. She put her hand up too late, and she whacked my neck. I missed the basket, and we tumbled to the floor.

While Jonesy Sawyer retrieved the ball, I headed to the top of the key. Reagan followed to defend me.

"Was that necessary?" I asked.

She shrugged. "Whoops."

Jonesy tossed me the ball.

"Whoops?"

"Come on, save the tea party for later," said Diggers.

"Play nice," I told Reagan.

We played hard. When our second winds ran out, we stopped and lined up at the water fountain.

Supervisor Andrew Walters cruised into the gym.

"Hey, you guys aren't supposed to be here without me," he said.

"The door was open," said Diggers. "And you were late."

"Yeah, yeah," said Andrew. "Just don't do it again." He pulled a *Sports Illustrated* out of his backpack and sat on the stage. He was on my brother's varsity team. Luke was a summer supervisor, too.

"Come on," said Reagan. "Let's go!"

We played for a good hour. A couple other kids showed up, so we had subs. But I didn't take a break, and I was dragging when we called it quits. A batch of older boys waited on the sidelines, and I was happy to hand over the court.

"Need one more," said their ringleader, John Rayfield, also on Luke's team. "Andrew, play?"

"Can't," he said. "Rules."

"Guys?" Rayfield looked at the boys walking off the floor, but they shook their heads.

"I'll play," said Reagan.

"You're nuts," I told her. "Time to call it quits."

"I need the practice."

"No, you don't," I said.

"I'm staying," Reagan said, bouncing the ball in place.

"Excellent," said Rayfield. "Play up top."

"Bad idea," I said.

"See you later," Reagan said.

I gave up. "Okay."

She kept dribbling as I walked away. I heard her patient style—bounce, two, three, bounce, two, three—all the way down the hall until I reached the outside door. Standing still, Reagan bounced the ball like she had all the time in the world.

Except it was my ball. I stopped in the parking lot and thought about running back to get it. Instead, I texted "Bring back my ball" to Reagan.

I headed home, stopping at the corner store for a root beer and a bag of chips. I walked through Elliot Park, and I wandered to the pool and stood outside its chain-link fence. The blond lifeguard yelled at some boys to stop doing cannonballs.

I breathed in the chlorinated air and sipped my drink.

Then one boy landed a can opener that soaked me. I didn't mind getting wet. It wasn't that hot, but I was still overheated from playing basketball.

The boy's friends followed suit, drenching the pool deck.

The lifeguard blew his whistle long and hard. The entire

pool grew quiet. Even the little kids in the wading pool stopped splashing. A siren wailed in the distance.

"You and you and you!" he yelled at the delinquents. "On the bench now!"

I smiled. Reagan and I had been benched for bringing a basketball in that pool a few years ago. I watched kids play in the water until my root beer was gone.

By the time I reached the house, I wasn't tired anymore. And it was too nice to go inside, so I decided to practice in the driveway.

I grabbed an old ball from the garage. I did sets of foul shots and broke them up with some crossover dribbling drills. Then I practiced quick-stop jump shots. And then I just shot baskets. I was still there when Mom drove home from the office.

And I was still there when she called me into the kitchen.

I stood inside the back door, holding the basketball against my hip. Mom's face was pale. Cell phone in one hand, she gripped the counter so tight her knuckles were white.

"Mom?"

"She just died," she said.

The hairs on my neck froze.

"Who?"

"I'm so sorry, Sam. They said she just died."

My heart pounded.

"Gram?' I asked.

Mom shook her head. Then she walked over and smoothed away the strand of hair that always escaped from my sweatband. Her fingers trembled.

"Mom, you're scaring me."

She looked at me as if she was memorizing my face.

"Mom, who died?" My voice shook.

She breathed deeply.

"Reagan."

My own breath stuck in my throat.

"She just died."

I dropped the ball. It bounced until it couldn't bounce anymore. And then it slowly rolled against the refrigerator. And stopped.

I was still there, but Reagan was gone.

BROKENHEARTED

We sat at the kitchen table.

"Tell me again," I said.

Mom put her hand on mine. She had told me twice already.

"Reagan's heart stopped," she said softly. "They think it was a congenital defect like maybe an enlarged heart. She was born with it, and she got big enough for it to give out. They won't know for sure until . . ." She hesitated.

"Until the autopsy," I said.

Mom closed her eyes.

"Until they see what's left of it."

"Sam," said Mom. Her eyes misted.

"We haven't grown since last winter," I said.

"It's something that catches up to you."

"I tried to make her stop playing and come with me," I said. "It's my fault."

"It is not!" Mom said. "You can't think like that, Sam."

"But if she had come with me—" I said.

"It might have happened on the way home," she said. "Or in the next game."

"I should have made her come with me."

Luke burst through the door. His face was red.

"Sam," he said. "I can't believe it." He gulped air. "I was at the Community Center when Andrew called Mr. Wheeler."

He sat beside me.

"What happened?" I asked.

He shook his head. "Reagan went for a rebound and then she was on the floor and she didn't get up."

"He was late," I said. "Andrew. And he left the door open."

"He couldn't find a pulse," said Luke.

"God," said Mom.

"He called 911 and ran for the defibrillator, you know, the one in the hall?"

The school system had installed one outside the gym entrance. Its glass door was dusty and someone kept putting a Grant Middle School Chargers sticker on it.

"He shocked Reagan once and then the ambulance guys ran in and they said she had a faint heartbeat and they rushed her to the hospital."

I remembered the siren at the pool. Oh God.

Luke shook his head. "I called Mrs. Murphy—I had her number in my phone from doing that yard work, remember, Mom? I told her they rushed Reagan to the hospital."

He bit his lip. "She asked, was it her knee?" He shook his

head. "I said I didn't think so." He looked at Mom. "I didn't know the right thing to say."

Mom grabbed his arm. "You did fine, Luke."

"She sprained her knee at camp," I said. "Just a little sprain and they iced it and she took it easy the next day."

"Then Mr. Wheeler and I picked up Andrew and we drove to the hospital," said Luke.

"There's a doctor at the camp all day long." Reagan resisted our coach's request that she get it examined, but you have no choice.

If she'd really messed up her knee, I would have been at her house, telling her about the pickup game and getting ready to watch TV and eat the popcorn that Mrs. Murphy always made us. Reagan said we had to work on our competitive edge when we were hurt, so we watched recorded games or sports movies. Reagan could recite the pep talk from the *Miracle on Ice* movie by heart.

Apparently, there weren't any miracles for her.

"They worked on her for a long time, but it was too late," Luke said. "There was too much damage." He took in a mouthful of air. "How can a kid have a heart attack?" He bit his lip and blinked fast.

When we were in fifth grade, Reagan told me that she was going to marry Luke when she turned thirty, if nothing better came along.

"And can't they fix hearts these days?" Luke asked.

"It was too late," said Mom. "The doctors think her heart was never right."

"I am so sorry, Sam," Luke said.

"Tell me again," I said.

Luke looked at me like I was crazy.

"Tell me what happened again," I said.

He shook his head.

"Her heart was too big, Sam," said Mom.

No, it wasn't. I reached to my neck and fingered my silver half heart on its chain. Reagan had the other half.

"Why didn't you call me?" I asked Luke.

"I did," he said.

"No, you didn't," I said.

It felt like everything was spinning around me. Then the front door opened, and Dad hurried into the kitchen. He walked over to my chair and hugged me.

And then I felt sick. I broke his grasp and ran for the bathroom and threw up the root beer and chips.

"Sweetie? You okay?" Mom said from outside the door.

"NO!" I yelled. I would never be okay again.

I sank to the floor and leaned against the wall. I didn't understand why I didn't get Luke's call.

Crap. I had left my phone in the garage.

I ran out of the bathroom and toward the garage, nearly knocking Mom down. I found my phone on top of the folded Ping-Pong table. Sure enough, Luke had called and texted "Call me ASAP."

But when I switched to my conversations with Reagan, all I had was the "Bring back my ball" request I had sent her. And that was it, since I had cleaned out my texts after finding

Bradley reading them last week. My only saved message with Reagan would be "Bring back my ball." And I'd never know if she had actually read it.

Bring back my ball. That was it. Bring back my ball.

THAT WILL BE FIVE CENTS, PLEASE

When I woke up the next morning and checked my phone, I couldn't believe it was ten o'clock. Usually, it would have vibrated itself off the night table with messages from Reagan if I wasn't up by eight. She was the only kid I knew who didn't need sleep. It made sleepovers exhausting.

But there were no messages.

Then reality struck. No more wake-up calls. No more Reagan.

I closed my eyes like that would make it all go away. I pulled the covers over my head. I pushed my head deep into the pillow, like I did when I was a little kid and didn't want a dream to stop. When I wanted some magical world to go on and on, sometimes a high-scoring basketball game where I couldn't miss, or an adventure in the tropics where Reagan and I would swim with the dolphins.

But nothing helped. It was like a thick, dark cloud had floated through the open window. Every molecule in the universe seemed intent on telling me personally that Reagan was gone.

I couldn't stand it. I pulled off the covers and went down-stairs.

"You're up," Mom said in the kitchen.

"You're here," I replied. Usually Mom left for her job as a city planner before I got up in the summer, first dropping off Bradley at day camp.

"Of course," she said.

I stumbled to the table.

"Want some cereal?" she asked.

"Not hungry," I said.

"Well, some orange juice, then."

"Mom."

She stared at me. "Right. You don't like orange juice." She shook her head. "I haven't been able to think straight." She reached out and hugged me for a long time. Then she sat.

"Look, the wake is tomorrow night, but you don't have to go," she said, "if that would be too much. The funeral is Saturday."

"That's convenient," I said.

She gave me a weird look.

I shrugged.

"Sam," she said. "There is a counselor at school—at Grant—for kids who want to talk to someone." She paused. "Not just Grant kids, any kid who might have known Reagan from the Y, or the Blizzard team, or school."

"That's nice," I said.

"I think we should go."

That made as much sense as eating breakfast.

"Why? It won't bring Reagan back."

"No, honey," she said. "Nothing will do that." She took a breath. "Your father and I are worried about you, and it wouldn't hurt to talk to a counselor."

"I don't want to talk to anyone," I said. "It won't help."

"Sam," Mom said. "Probably not. But it would make me feel better." She hesitated. "I don't feel like I'm at my best right now." She started to cry. "And I love you and I want to help you through this the best way I can."

That hit the heartstrings. Mom sometimes said thank God for Reagan so she could pretend she had two daughters to go with her two sons.

"Okay," I said. "I'll go."

I stood in front of my closet. Reagan and I had nearly completed our freshman year wardrobes, between twice-weekly jaunts to the mall and regular stops at Vintage Discounts on Main Street. Reagan decided the focus should be subjects, so I had outfits for biology, geometry, and world history. Biology had green and pastels, geometry was minimalist with prints with squares and circles, and history was a skirt and embroidered blouse. I hadn't worn a skirt or dress all through middle school, but I was going to step up my act in high school.

I didn't know what you were supposed to wear to visit a counselor about your dead friend.

It was so overwhelming that I just put on basketball shoes to go with the shorts I had slept in and grabbed a sweatshirt from the floor. Mom didn't even object when I showed up downstairs without combing my hair.

"Come on," she said.

I didn't want to go. But I didn't have the energy to put up a fight. I was on autopilot, where you're alive but you don't really know what you are doing. So it wasn't until Mom had pulled into a parking space and we walked into the building that I realized that I was at Grant. The counseling for Reagan's death was at the place she had died. How stupid.

Mom caught the same thought when we walked down the corridor with the doors to the gym. I stopped.

"Sam," Mom said.

I pulled on the door handle. It swung open.

The gym was empty. No summer camp on grief-counseling days. Morning sun filtered down from the high, narrow windows. I walked to midcourt and my heart sped up when I imagined what had happened. I looked at the basket near the entrance. And then I looked at the basket near the stage. And I imagined Reagan going up against the high school players for a rebound, reaching for the ball, and collapsing. And I saw Andrew jump from the stage. And run for the defibrillator. And I saw the paramedics rush in and take Reagan away on a gurney.

At least her last good heartbeats were on a basketball court. She would have been so mad if they were in a classroom.

And that's when I saw my ball in the corner, sitting on top of Reagan's blue Nike hoodie. I walked over and stood still for a few minutes, wondering if I should say a prayer. Instead,

I carried the hoodie and ball to center court and sat down. I felt Reagan's cell phone in the sweatshirt pocket. Carefully wrapped around it was her half-heart chain.

The phone still had juice.

We used the same passcode. My hands shaking, I typed it in.

The home screen lit up.

Reagan had received the text about bringing my ball back. She replied, but she didn't hit Send.

"Good thing you've got me!" she'd typed.

I hit Send.

And that's when I cried for the first time. Mom's heels clicked across the floor, and she wrapped her arms around me and my basketball and Reagan's hoodie. And I cried harder. Or my body cried. Like it said, "You may not have absorbed this news about Reagan, but I have—and my tear ducts are full and I'm going to run a channel of tears right down your cheeks. And I'm going to do it for quite some time."

We never got to the counselor's office.

FUNERAL

I think I went to the wake. I think my parents told me I didn't have to go and I said I had to go and I went but it was all so incredibly horrible, the very idea of it, that I don't remember if I actually went or if it was the nightmare about it that I remembered. A hundred different versions that woke me up again and again last night.

I sat like a zombie at the funeral. I couldn't have told you who I was or where I was. I was simply occupying my body. Like a zombie. I sat like that until Bradley farted. Not like a normal fart that you might get away with outdoors but is mortifying in church. This one sounded like it couldn't possibly be produced by a human being, never mind a nine-year-old boy. It sounded like a bomb. I glanced at Bradley, who had this look of amazement on his face.

I burst out laughing. And then I laughed at the fact that I was laughing at Reagan's funeral. I couldn't stop laughing, and I laughed so hard that I had to hold my stomach. And then I realized that if I was laughing at Reagan's funeral, I would never laugh with her again.

And then I started to cry. It was me this time, not just my tear ducts. And I couldn't stop crying. I cried so hard that I was shaking, and I took big gulps of air because there wasn't any left inside me. And I cried and I wailed and I gulped, and I didn't care who heard me or who saw me because it was Reagan's funeral.

It was true. Reagan was gone. And there was no going back to her being alive.

The last thing I remember about Reagan's funeral was being carried down the aisle by both Mom and Dad, and Mom saying, "Oh, honey," and Dad saying, "Breathe, Sam, you have to breathe."

OH, BROTHER

I sat at the table, sipping my instant breakfast. I didn't feel like eating, but Mom claimed I'd lost weight since Reagan died, so I promised I would drink an instant breakfast each morning. I sipped it slowly to put off my assigned chore of loading the breakfast dishes into the dishwasher.

"You're kidding," said Luke around ten.

I looked up from reading the box of Cheerios.

Luke wore basketball shorts and his faded YMCA T-shirt, his arm around his basketball.

"What?" I asked.

"How can you sit there for so long?"

I shrugged.

"Come play," he said.

I shook my head. "I'm not finished," I said. I pointed at my half-empty glass.

He ignored me. "Come on," he said.

"Why aren't you at work?" I asked.

"Who are you, the police?"

I narrowed my eyes. Both Mom and Dad had taken vacation days to stay home with me. But I just wanted to be alone.

"It's not about you," Luke said. "We have budget cuts, which means we have to take a day off every other week. It sucks." He motioned me up. "So come out and play with me."

I shook my head.

I couldn't imagine playing ball without Reagan.

"Then just rebound," he said. "Stand in the sun and catch a few balls, okay?"

"I don't have my shoes on," I said. I returned to my box of Cheerios.

"Woman, I am not your manservant." But he walked to the stairs, pounding out each and every step, and returned with my basketball shoes.

"But . . ." I said, pointing at my bare feet.

He pulled out a sock from each shoe.

"I don't want to play," I said.

Luke tossed the shoes and socks into my lap. "Just come outside. And then we can tell Mom and Dad you're working out again and they'll get off your back."

He had a point. You'd think my parents had turned into the personal trainers on infomercials the way they kept telling me that I would feel better with exercise.

I would never feel better.

"Come on," said Luke.

I followed him to the driveway. It had been so long since

I'd been outside that the sun was blinding. I had to shade my eyes.

Luke laughed. "You're like the groundhog who's come out to check on spring."

I glared at him with my hand still half covering my eyes.

Luke bounced the ball a few times and shot it through the net. He retrieved it and passed it to me.

I held on to it. "I'm not playing. I'm only rebounding."

"Whatever," he said. "Ready?"

I nodded and stood under the basket. It was a nice morning with soft sun and chirping birds. But something about it seemed unreal, too. Like I'd wandered into a parallel universe that was like mine but it wasn't mine.

Luke stood at the white stripe he'd painted on the driveway for the foul line.

"Ready?"

"Are you ready?" I asked. I folded my arms.

He sighed. But he shot the basketball. It swished.

I let it bounce a couple times, and then I tossed it back to him.

Luke got set again. He squared himself, looked at the rim, pursed his lips, and then gently released the ball, following through with his right hand. Using exactly the same routine, he made ten baskets in a row.

"Are you sure you don't want in?" he said. "This much perfection could be mind-numbing."

I shook my head.

"Okay."

Luke proceeded to take ten more shots, making baskets with eight of them, running through his paces like clockwork.

I was in a routine myself, letting the ball bounce once before I picked it up, taking one step forward as I made a two-handed chest pass back to Luke and stepping back into position. It took more energy than reading the Cheerios box, but it was at the same level of difficulty.

Luke lined up again, but this time he deliberately missed, clanging the right side of the rim so the ball skipped past my reach and rolled into the hedges.

"Very funny," I said. I strolled to the ball.

"Making sure you can still move," Luke said.

"Play right or I'm going inside."

"You're going to a shrink if you don't start acting normal."

"What?"

"Seriously, Sam," said Luke, his hands on his hips. "Mom and Dad are looking for someone. They're really worried."

"It's only been two weeks," I said. "Since."

"I know," Luke said. "And I know it's awful."

I tossed him the ball. "Shoot your stupid free throws."

"Play a little one-on-one," said Luke. "Like we used to. I'll spot you five."

"I don't want to play."

"Fine. Then go to a shrink. That will be more fun."

"Screw you," I said. I turned for the steps.

Luke hit me in the back with the ball.

"What are you doing?" I yelled.

I picked up the basketball and threw it back. Hard. He

grabbed it and fired it at me. I caught it even though it stung my hands.

"Fine!" I said. "You want to play—we'll play!"

I dribbled beyond the foul line, bounced the ball twice, and then drove right at Luke, elbowing him with my left arm as I made a layup with my right hand.

"So we're fouling," he said.

"Wasn't a foul," I said.

"Right."

I took the ball outside again. He pretended to guard me. I faked right and drove left. He let me go, and I made an easy layup from the left side.

"I thought you wanted to play ball, not nursemaid," I said.

"Just letting you warm up," he said.

"Warm," I said.

"Okay."

I dribbled the ball in place for a few seconds, pounding it fast against the pavement. Luke moved up and swiped at it. I turned around and backed into him, still dribbling. He reached around and tried to take the ball away. I shoved my hip into him.

"Incidental contact," I said.

"Imbecile contact, you mean," Luke said.

I pushed him away and backed off a few steps. But he guarded me closely again, putting his hand on my back.

"Incidental contact," he said.

"Not funny," I said.

I stepped left, and then I stepped right, and then I took two steps back and launched a long jump shot. It clanged against the front rim and I leaped for the rebound, along with the six-foot-three Luke. I got a hand on it, but he got both hands on it. He and I and the ball crashed to the driveway. Luke landed on my left arm, and my foot got caught under his stomach.

"Get off me!" I yelled.

Luke jumped up. "Your arm okay?"

I shook it. It hurt. "It's great," I said. "My ball."

"What?"

I took the ball outside again.

"Come on," I said. I motioned weakly with my throbbing left hand.

"You should put some ice on that," Luke said.

"Come on!"

He shook his head. But he took a few steps toward me and positioned his hand to guard me.

I was so angry I couldn't see straight. I started toward the basket and then pulled up and sank a jump shot. Luke got the ball and tossed it back. He said nothing. I dribbled a couple times, and then I pulled up and launched another. Swish. Luke retrieved the ball again.

I caught Luke's toss and felt the pebbled surface of the basketball in my hands. Gripping it was second nature to them. And I did what was second nature to me—I glanced down the street, looking for Reagan.

I reached up and felt the half hearts. I had added Reagan's to my chain.

The two halves that weren't making a whole.

I pounded the ball on the driveway. Once. Twice. Three times. I couldn't believe that I was there and Reagan was six feet under.

"Sam?" asked Luke.

Reagan was supposed to come flying around the corner on her bike, her ball in one arm, yelling, "Wait for me!" at the top of her lungs.

Reagan was supposed to be playing with me. But now Luke was helping me stay out of a shrink's office because Reagan was dead, and apparently I was taking it badly. Because I missed my best friend forever and the forever part had been a total lie. It wasn't even until high school.

"Sam?" asked Luke.

I narrowed my eyes and stared at my stupid brother. Already sweating like a horse, he stood with his monster hands by his sides, his outgrown T-shirt squeezed over his bulging biceps. He was so not Reagan.

I dropped the ball and charged him. He was so surprised that I knocked him to the ground. I pummeled his chest with punches.

He was not Reagan. I wanted Reagan. And he was not Reagan.

Luke grabbed my right arm. I whacked him with my left arm until he grabbed that, too. He rolled me over.

"Cut it out!" I screamed. "Let me go!"

"Then stop hitting me!" yelled Luke.

He let go, and I roundhoused him. He grabbed me again, and we tumbled over and over across the driveway and onto the grass, where he pinned me to the ground.

"Let me up!" I screamed.

"Not until you promise to cool off!"

I struggled against him, kicking when I couldn't budge his arms.

"Ouch!" said Luke. "Stop it!"

"Get off me!" I yelled. "So help me, I'll bite you!"

"You wouldn't dare!" said Luke. He pressed me down harder.

"Okay, okay, uncle!" I screamed.

Luke released his grip and closed his eyes and took a deep breath.

I reached behind me to a half-opened bag of fertilizer and grabbed a handful. But just when I started to throw it at Luke, he saw me.

He grabbed my wrists and pinned me down once more. The fertilizer fell out of my hand.

"Calm down, Sam!" he yelled.

Dad pulled into the driveway for lunch. He rolled down the window.

"What in tarnation is going on?" he yelled. He opened the door. "Get off her, Luke!"

Luke rolled off and sat beside me. I closed my eyes, wanting only to sink below the grass. I wanted to be deep down in the ground with Reagan.

"Sam, are you okay?" asked Dad.

I lay there with my eyes closed.

"She's fine, Dad," said Luke.

"Then why isn't she getting up?"

Luke said something else to Dad, but I had stopped paying attention.

Dad all but carried me to my room. I slept until supper.

LOST IN PLACE

A week later, I lay in bed, resting after finishing my instant breakfast and loading the dishes. My daily routine now had an afternoon phase—working at the Recreation Department sports day camp. I herded nine-year-olds from one sport to another, keeping a head count so I didn't lose anyone. I'm not sure why anyone thought it was a good fit, since I'd forgotten to walk Bradley to his orthodontist appointment. The choice was to see a therapist or prove that I was feeling better by rejoining the world, as Mom put it.

I sighed.

I looked around my room. There was no view without reminders of Reagan: the Dribble Queen picture; my Junior Olympics first-place ribbon for the hundred-yard dash because we switched off and Reagan ran (and won) the fifty-yard dash; the height marks for us that crawled up the side of the closet doorframe. The last set was exactly the same—five feet eight inches. A red-ringed ceramic cup from Reagan's tea set sat on my bureau, glued back together after I had knocked it down dribbling in her room. We had never returned it to its native habitat.

A breeze riffled my drapes.

I smiled. The last time we had used the set was after Reagan won the Dribble Queen contest. We served ourselves lemonade and cookies and pretended to conduct the player draft for the WNBA. Reagan said that winning the Dribble Queen made her the top pick. I reluctantly agreed and accepted the number two slot. Trades put us both on the Washington Mystics. Their initials, WM, were perfect for Samantha Wilson and Reagan Murphy. We loved that our last-name initials were upside-down versions of each other.

A train whistle blew in the distance.

It's not like outside was any better. Reagan and I had played sports all over town. Last summer we invented the Tour de Spalding, riding our bikes to every public court and shooting baskets or playing a little one-on-one at each stop. And several years before that was the infamous Tour de Vanilla, when we rode our bikes to every place that served ice cream. Our stomachs were so upset by the time we completed our mission at the Dairy Queen that we had to call Mom to pick us up.

I laughed out loud. Reagan claimed she was going to buy the chain when she became a famous WNBA star and rename it Dribble Queen.

I felt the half hearts. We were supposed to be doing this together.

I reached for the phone on my nightstand. I thumbed to our last conversation.

"Good thing you've got me!"

My heart skipped a beat. I grabbed my pillow tight.

I didn't know what I was supposed to do without her.

I had news for people who say that life goes on.

It doesn't.

NOT TODAY

"You have to go to school," said Mom.

"No, I don't."

She sat on the side of my bed. "I know how hard this is for you."

"No, you don't."

"You're right," she said. "I can't possibly know."

I said nothing. I couldn't explain the feeling that my life's plan had been fed through a shredder.

My heart pounded. I sucked in some air.

Mom put her arm around me. "Oh, honey," she said. "I know how badly you miss Reagan. I know that."

I nodded. I felt the tears well up again.

"But you're going to have to go back to school," she said. "If not today, then tomorrow."

"Not today," I said.

Mom sighed. "Okay. You can miss the first day of school."

I closed my eyes and tried to go back to sleep.

BACK TO SCHOOL

At the breakfast table, I stared longingly at the TV and the couch in the family area. I had watched a marathon session of *Law & Order* yesterday. Two episodes involved truancy, which must have counted for something.

Mom noticed and shook her head.

I took a deep breath, sipped the rest of my instant breakfast, and climbed the stairs to dress for school.

My clothes were laid out on my bed like I was in first grade. The black capris with the navy-squares-print blouse. Mom must have thought I couldn't get past my closet. I sighed. But I didn't care what I wore, so I threw them on, found my black Sperrys, brushed my hair, and headed back downstairs.

"You didn't have to do that, you know," I told Mom, who was standing at the kitchen sink.

"What?"

"Put my clothes out. I'm not a basket case."

She looked at me like I was crazy.

Whatever.

"Give me a hug." Mom pointed at the door. "Your brother's waiting in his truck."

I hugged her tight.

I got into the truck and slammed the passenger door shut.

Luke backed down the driveway and turned into the street. He looked terrible. He hadn't shaved and his T-shirt was a dead ringer for what he wore last night.

I stared at him.

"Calculus," he said.

He drove through Broad Street and sped down Stark Road to Carlow High.

"In a hurry?" I asked. Bad enough I had to go, I didn't see a reason for rushing.

I still couldn't imagine school without Reagan. I tried to shut off the thinking. I just needed to put one Sperry in front of the other.

Luke parked his truck next to the soccer field, in the marked space farthest from the school building. That meant a lot of Sperry steps.

"How's this different from walking to school?" I asked.

Luke grunted. "I didn't make you ride with me," he said. "I need to keep the truck safe from student drivers."

I shook my head.

I put my hand on the door handle, but I couldn't make myself work it. Luke came around and opened it.

"You'll be okay," he said.

I didn't feel okay. But I stepped out of the truck.

He pulled out my backpack and handed it to me. We walked silently to the gym entrance, and I stayed close to him as we walked down the back hall. He bopped me in the arm before heading to his locker. "Hey, text me if you need anything," he said.

I nodded.

I stood at the counter outside the administration offices, feeling incredibly alone.

"Wow, no one misses the first day," said the gray-haired woman helping me. Her name tag said she was Mrs. Jenkins. The principal, Mr. Carson, stood in his doorway. He sent a sympathetic nod my way.

"Unless you are excused because of a big music competition or travel delays from a church mission in South America," said Mrs. Jenkins. "That happened last year."

I shook my head. "Nothing like that."

"Then you must have caught a bad summer cold," Mrs. Jenkins said. "Summer colds can be miserable."

I shook my head again.

"Oh," she said. She stared at me like the only other explanation was that I was from outer space and had mistimed my intergalactic journey.

"Reagan's dead," I said.

"Excuse me?"

"Reagan kept me on schedule, but she's dead now."

"Oh," she said.

The be-nice-to-dead-Reagan's-best-friend movement hadn't made it to the office.

"I keep waiting for her to show up and tell me where to go, but she's dead."

"Oh," she said. "Oh dear."

That got her moving. She pulled out a manila folder with my schedule. "Now, you should have received this information in email and regular mail, but . . ."

"We took the same classes, Reagan and me," I said. "I used to let her handle those details."

"Of course you did," she said.

"I read the reading list books," I said. "But Reagan didn't."

"Good for you," she said.

But she had a strange look that said that nobody actually read the freshman reading list. It seemed that I was the only kid on earth who didn't know that.

"She didn't like classes, either, but she was always on time."

"Good for her," she said. Then she put her hand to her mouth. "I mean, I'm sorry for your loss."

"Thank you," I said. I turned and headed to the classrooms.

"Best of luck," called out Mr. Carson. "Welcome to Carlow High."

Oh, that would make everything okay.

I missed Reagan more than ever when I saw the desks and chairs in Spanish class, even though this was a new school that had never known her. I took a back-row seat after introducing myself to the teacher, Señora Somebody, and I searched for familiar faces. A couple guys were from my grade at Grant, but I couldn't remember their names. The girl next to me gave me a thin smile, and I gave her a thin smile back.

And then I bit my lip to stop from crying. I wanted to go home. But I decided I should wait to contact Luke until I was closer to a full-scale breakdown. I bit my lip harder and tried to pay attention. They must have gone into overdrive yesterday because Señora spoke mostly in Spanish and my classmates seemed to understand.

I tried to listen, but I felt like I was the only one who didn't know the secret handshake. I kept telling myself they were saying stuff like "hello" and "good-bye" and "how are you?" but I couldn't pick it up.

A kid stuck his head in the doorway and got Señora's attention. He handed her a piece of paper. And then Señora said my name and motioned me to come to the front of the room. She handed me the note, which said *Mr. Offerman's office. Room 100B.*

I looked at Señora.

"Take your things with you," she said.

She seemed glad to see me go.

The sign on room 100B, part of the administration suite, was "Guidance." I figured college applications wasn't the topic. So much for avoiding a counselor's office. I could have been at home, watching more *Law & Order*.

I sighed. And knocked.

"Come in."

Mr. Offerman looked like he coached the offensive line

when classes weren't in session. His belt could handle two skinny guys like my dad. I sat across from him.

"I understand you've had a great loss," he said. His voice was incredibly deep.

I nodded.

"My deepest sympathies," he said.

He would be a great undertaker if the coaching didn't work out.

I nodded again.

"I worked as a crisis counselor at Grant this summer, you know . . ."

"When Reagan died," I said. "Reagan Murphy."

He nodded. "And I understand it was difficult to start school again without your friend."

Thanks, Mom, I thought.

"Her name was Reagan," I said. "And she was my best friend."

"I wanted to touch base and let you know I'm here to help with that transition."

I didn't say anything.

"Make an appointment and we can talk about your feelings and help you adjust."

He looked straight at me. Kindly. And I looked past him to the clock on the wall. The second hand pushed time to the nine o'clock bell.

It rang. I stood.

"Thank you, Mr. Offerman."

"Anytime," he said.

I could barely breathe when I walked out of his office. It was all I could do to head up the hall to my next class, geometry. I was just trying to get through the day, and it felt like I was playing some online game with scary pop-ups. I stopped at the doorway to collect myself. I was the last one to take my seat, next to some goth boy decked out completely in black, from his scuffed-up Doc Martens to his fake black hair. I wondered if he was in mourning for someone like Reagan or the world at large.

Goth Boy looked up from drawing in his notebook and smiled at me.

I sat back in the chair, armed with that smile and Luke's phone number, and I steeled myself to make it through one more class.

I have pretty good hearing, but what I did hear from Mr. Pratt, the teacher, was mumbled. And that's when he stopped looking at his shoes. The only time he acted like a teacher was when he asked a question that wasn't about math. Then he stood straight and tall and barked out the question like he was a drill sergeant. It was like he had dueling personalities, and neither one was appealing.

Goth Boy was one of his first targets. After mumbling the lesson, Mr. Pratt asked him to tell him the difference between a line segment and a ray. Goth Boy looked at him like why would he do that since Mr. Pratt had just spent fifteen minutes showing the difference between a line segment and a ray with multiple sketches on the whiteboard.

Mr. Pratt shook his head after Goth Boy produced no sounds for a good minute. He moved to Brian Dowling, a friend of Luke's who should have been way past geometry, and asked the same question.

Brian was clueless. I understood why his nickname was Brain D.

I flipped through the textbook during class, hoping that it would teach me what I needed to learn all by itself, once we moved beyond the line segment and the ray.

I hesitated at the beginning of the lunch line. Of all the things that would be hard without Reagan, you wouldn't think it would be getting crappy food in a crappy school cafeteria. But she was such a chatterbox that I guess I never thought about what I was doing with the silverware and the napkins—never mind figuring out what I wanted to eat. Maybe Reagan had picked out food for both of us. I felt like a little kid dumbstruck her first time at a McDonald's counter.

"Sam!" Maddie and Jonesy stood in front of me. I hadn't seen them since I walked into the funeral. I grimaced, thinking of the last time they saw me, getting lugged out of there. Great.

"How are you?" asked Maddie. She hugged me.

I didn't hug her back.

Jonesy put an arm around me. "We get why you didn't call us back—no problem—but we have been thinking about you."

"Thanks."

I should have returned their calls. They were trying to help, like I did when Jonesy had mono in seventh grade and

I delivered her homework with fresh chocolate chip cookies every day.

"It's hard, you know?" I said.

"Sure," said Jonesy. "It's so awful."

"I can't even think about it," said Maddie.

I can't not think about it, I thought.

"My mom said that getting back into a school routine would help everyone."

I nodded. But I so disagreed. Today was hell.

"Eat with us, okay?" asked Maddie.

"Cool."

We found a table in the middle of the huge cafeteria. Maddie and Jonesy talked about their classes and some guy named Rick Roberts, and I listened in a robotic sort of way and played with my grilled cheese and applesauce. But I wanted to compare notes with Reagan and find out what she thought about Señora Somebody and whether geometry teacher Mr. Pratt would mumble all year or whether actual math words would come out of his mouth.

"Sam?" asked Maddie.

"Sorry," I said. "What did you say?"

"Are you going out for a sport this fall?" she asked. "You're such a good athlete."

I shook my head.

Mom had brought the tryout literature from school to my room and told me how good it would be for me. How it would keep me busy and I would meet new people and some cross-training would be great for my basketball. And I was such a good athlete that I could probably make a team in a sport I hadn't played for years.

"Saving yourself for basketball?" Maddie asked.

I shrugged. No need to let the world know that my basketball career was history. I had no desire to play without Reagan.

"That's cool," said Jonesy.

I took a deep breath. It took all the guts I had to perk up and appear interested. "What about you guys?"

"Soccer," said Maddie. "I'll wind up subbing, but that's fine with me."

"But you made the team? That's great," I said. "I'll come watch."

No, I wouldn't.

"And I'm running cross-country," said Jonesy. "They take everybody. I figure that's one way to work on my fitness."

Jonesy's athletic advantage was her height. Reagan always said she loped down the court like she was trying to mount a horse that wouldn't stand still. The image of a horse running with the cross-country team made me smile.

"What's so funny, Reagan?" Maddie asked.

My face turned cold. I sat straight up.

Jonesy poked Maddie.

"Oh, yeah, sorry, Sam. You two, well, you were always together."

"We're not together now, are we?" I said.

That was so nasty I felt the knife myself.

"She didn't mean it," said Jonesy.

I took a deep breath. "I know," I said. "I'm sorry."

"No, I'm sorry," said Maddie. She started to reach for my shoulder, but I leaned away.

"We all miss her," said Jonesy.

"I still can't believe you and I were playing pickup with her just fine, and she's joking around when we all left, and then . . ." said Maddie. She wiped a tear from her eye. "I can't believe it."

"I know," I said.

But I didn't know. Jonesy and Maddie played basketball with us and clowned around before practices and came along on some Saturday adventures. But they had no idea what I was missing. They had no idea how it felt when your best friend vanished. They had no idea of the aching hole it left inside you and how it grew every single day when you realized more and more what you would be missing the rest of your life.

I breathed faster.

All the memories-to-be from high school with Reagan flooded into my brain so fast that it felt like a dam burst. Uncountable memories from the hallways and the cafeteria and the math classrooms roared through my head.

Uncountable memories from the gym.

My pulse throbbed in my neck.

I grabbed my tray and stood.

"Gotta go," I blurted to Maddie and Jonesy.

I bit my lip to stop the tears. I unloaded my tray and hurried out of the cafeteria. I ran down the first floor hall and tossed my books in my locker. I texted Luke as I walked out the back entrance.

"Need to leave. Waiting at truck."

I walked past stretching phys ed students. The sun was bright, and they were chattering away like blue jays.

I walked faster, concentrating on moving the Sperrys to the truck so I could close the door on the whole depressing scene. But when I pulled on the handle, it was locked.

Come on, Luke, really?

That was the final straw. I slumped to the ground, my back against the door. I put my head in my hands and sobbed.

A few minutes later, I felt a hand on my shoulder.

"Hey," said Luke. He squatted beside me.

My sobbing slowed to a whimper.

"I cried the first time I had Mr. Pratt, too," said Luke.

I laughed through my sniffles.

"Come on, let's get you home."

"Will you get in trouble?" I asked.

He shook his head. "Told the front office you were throwing up," he said. "They really don't like vomit."

"I feel like throwing up," I said.

Luke guided me into the passenger side.

"I know what you mean," he said.

When we pulled into the driveway, Mom's car was there.

"Really?" I said.

He shrugged.

But when Mom opened the door and opened her arms, I ran to be in them, and I cried on her shoulder.

COME SATURDAY MORNING

I woke up slowly on Saturday morning.

I had made it through the rest of school that week. I clutched my phone the entire time, calming myself with the thought that I could quickly text Luke for an escape. Even though Mom had probably told him that I had to stick it out, I knew my brother would come through. He could stash me at the mall until school let out.

I rolled over. Even the smell of Mom's pancakes didn't move me from under the covers. And neither did the stack of books on my desk and the reading assignments that I had put off until the weekend.

I fingered the half hearts, so sad that I would never see Reagan's bouncing against her neck again as we rode our bikes or played basketball in the driveway. I needed to hear her voice so bad it was killing me.

The sun squeezed between the drapes. I pulled the covers over my head.

"Good morning, high school girl!" said Dad. "Can I come in?"

I groaned. "Yes," I croaked.

I checked my phone. 10:30 a.m. Not even noon.

Dad opened the door. "I thought it would take until sophomore year to pick up Luke's sleeping habits," he said.

"I'm a quick learner," I said.

"Good," he said. "Because I need someone to help pick out flowers for the container pots on the front porch."

"Me? Now I'm some flower girl?"

"Yes, you."

"And this isn't a ploy to get me out of bed?"

"No," Dad said. "That was your mom's pancakes two hours ago."

"I wondered," I said. "Any left?"

"In the freezer."

"What, for breakfast Popsicles?"

Dad shrugged. "Don't knock 'em until you've tried them."

I smiled.

"We'll get you something to eat on the way to the garden center."

In a few minutes, Dad pulled into Polly's Donut Shop, one of the banned locales along with fast-food restaurants after Mom decided to improve our diets this year.

"Dad," I said.

"Don't tell. What do you want?"

The dark chocolate cake donut might have been the first

food that tasted good in weeks. I inhaled it so quickly that Dad went back inside and bought two more. After we licked our fingers and destroyed the evidence, we took on the garden center. I helped pick out enough asters and stonecrops to fill Mom's pots as well as those of several neighbors.

An hour later, I was back on my bed, staring at the stack of books on my desk. I didn't know what to do. I didn't feel like doing anything, but when I tried to come up with things to do that I could then reject, I struck out. I wondered if Reagan had decided what we did and I went along with it.

It was Saturday. Reagan and I used to go to Saturday movie matinees, sometimes taking Bradley to the second-run movie theater downtown. But I always got restless an hour into it. And God forbid if I started whispering to Reagan, who soaked in every line of dialogue and did NOT want that interrupted. Which seemed so at odds with her nonstop talking self.

Jonesy loved movies almost as much as Reagan did. Maybe I could call Jonesy and see if she was interested. I grabbed my laptop and started to pull up the theater listings, but then I stopped. Sitting in a dark theater the rest of the afternoon was probably not a great idea.

And that sounded exactly like what Mom would say.

Great. I couldn't even come up with my own opinion of my lousy idea. I had to channel my mother.

Maybe Reagan did run our lives.

This was all too hard. I shucked off my shoes and pulled the covers over me.

"Samantha?" Mom called through the door.

I broke out of a dream about the flowers in the pots multiplying and surrounding the house. All that fresh air must have exhausted me.

"Yes?"

"Can I come in?"

"Yes."

"Are you sick?" she asked.

"No," I said.

She pulled open the drapes.

"What did you do that for?" I asked.

"Inviting the beautiful day into your room."

"Thank you," I said. "I think."

I swung my feet over the side of the bed. I checked my phone. I'd slept until three o'clock.

"What's on for the rest of the day?" Mom asked.

"Lunch, I guess," I said. "And then, you know, resting from school."

"Right," said Mom. "Anything else?"

"I thought about a movie," I said.

"And?"

"I decided not to go to a movie," I said.

"Would you like to go grocery shopping with me?" she asked.

"No thank you."

Mom looked frustrated. "Are you sure?"

I nodded.

"I do have a lot of homework," I said. "It would probably be a good idea to get started on that."

Mom looked encouraged. "Okay, then. Any requests from the store?"

I shook my head.

"Call me if you need anything, okay?"

I nodded.

She left and I pulled the covers over my head. Again.

Dad dragged me out of the house that night to go to a minor-league baseball game in Mansfield. The Wildcats were playing the Portland Sea Dogs in the last regular game of the year, and Dad liked to keep tabs on the upcoming Red Sox players. The stack of schoolbooks was getting on my nerves, and I went to escape them.

I sat next to Dad, who scored like he always did, and nibbled from my box of popcorn. The game was boring. Until the fourth inning, when I saw a dead ringer for Reagan walk down the aisle of the third-base stands. But I got distracted by a foul ball heading our way, and I didn't see where she sat down. I stared across the infield for the next two innings. Then I made bathroom and Coke runs, keeping an eye out in the concourse, and I stood at the top of the third-base stands and studied the rows beneath me.

After the seventh-inning stretch, I systematically examined

all the fans in the third-base stands—row by row, seat by seat. I had worked through each section twice without seeing Reagan again, when the game ended. Nothing.

One, two, three strikes you're out at the old ball game.

HELLO AGAIN

When Luke drove us into the parking lot Monday morning, the hope that school would get easier flew out the window. If the steering wheel had been in my hands, I would have turned the car around and returned home. I tried to be brave when I turned the corner to the freshman lockers. But the sound of my locker slamming shut like a prison door made me realize I was only a few weeks into a life sentence without Reagan.

Since you had one week to turn an unofficial absence into an official absence, I walked to the administration offices with the absence form signed by Mom for missing the first day of school and the afternoon of the second day of school. This time, Mrs. Jenkins was fully informed. She put her hand on mine after I gave her the paperwork and said, "We're all thinking about you, dear."

I kept my eyes peeled on the ground as I headed to Spanish. I didn't want to see anyone, never mind talk to anyone. In class, I scribbled something about forgetting to bring my book home on the vocabulary quiz. I hadn't touched a single book all weekend.

In geometry, Mr. Pratt waited for the bell to ring before he pointed at the two quiz questions on the board. Goth Boy stared at me when I pulled the same forgot-my-books move in geometry as in Spanish. I sat back in my chair while my classmates sighed about the problems. They scribbled their best shots. When Mr. Pratt loudly said "Time's up," I realized again that he spoke clearly enough when the topic wasn't mathematics.

Pratt motioned for us to pass in the quizzes. I handed mine to Brain D., who looked at me oddly like even he had written down a few possibilities. When he had collected all the quizzes and filed them in a manila folder, Mr. Pratt folded his arms and looked straight at Goth Boy.

"Why don't you tell us your solutions?" he asked.

It seemed that Mr. Pratt had found his project for the year.

Goth Boy shrugged. For whatever reason, he wasn't interested in classroom participation.

"Excuse me, sir?" said Mr. Pratt.

Goth Boy did not respond.

"We use words in this classroom."

Not well, I thought.

Goth Boy shook his head.

Mr. Pratt's face grew red. "One last chance," he said.

Goth Boy didn't change the empty expression on his face.

"That's it," said Mr. Pratt. "Detention this afternoon."

I prayed that Mr. Pratt wasn't directing his interrogation to me next because I truly couldn't answer the question. I had the feeling that Goth Boy could. But Pratt looked past Brain D. and me and collected his answers from a talkative math whiz named Angie.

When I walked into the cafeteria, I found Maddie and Jonesy waiting by the line. I guess they thought we were an official lunch group. More likely, Mom had asked that Maddie keep an eye on me during unsupervised periods. Especially when sharp objects like forks and knives were involved.

Maybe that's why none of my teachers had raised a stink about my lack of work so far. My sudden exit last week put me on a special student alert list. Make sure she's not sticking pills into her mouth and don't let her have scissors.

I nodded at Maddie and Jonesy. They smiled, I smiled, and we got into line.

Thinking of scissors made me think of kindergarten with Reagan. Ms. Olsen was obsessed with safety. We recited "no running with scissors" each morning after the Pledge of Allegiance after some kid had nearly impaled himself. So I thought the final line was "with liberty and justice for all and no running with scissors." I said it that way until halfway through first grade, when Ms. Remmick made us recite the pledge individually so she could figure out the murmur at the end of the class recitation.

Reagan never let me forget, regularly reminding me not to run with scissors. Sometimes, she whispered it right before an important free throw so I would laugh and loosen up.

I giggled.

"What's so funny?" asked Maddie.

"Oh, just something I remembered."

"Ah," said Jonesy. She touched my arm and smiled.

The lunch gang was definitely a watch group engineered by Mom.

Unbelievable.

"Tell us," said Maddie.

"That's okay," I said. "Just something from a long time ago."

They exchanged those about-Reagan looks I was starting to spot from a mile away.

I concentrated on the lunch selections. I chose a burrito. Then I got overwhelmed and grabbed the chocolate milk because I couldn't decide between lemonade and water. I took an extra knife for kicks.

Maddie looked at Jonesy, and Jonesy looked at Maddie.

When we found a table, I stared at my tray, trying to convince myself that chocolate and salsa complemented each other. Then I examined both knives and picked out the shiniest one. They should create a separate lunch menu for the depressed kids. Only finger foods like hamburgers and tacos and french fries and apples. Nothing that required sharp objects like knives and forks.

I laughed again.

Maddie and Jonesy exchanged concerned looks. They had signed up to support a friend, not guard a lunatic.

"What did you do this weekend?" asked Maddie.

"Nothing," I said. I picked up the fork and my chosen knife and cut the burrito into pieces. "No, that's not right. I helped my dad pick out flowers for these pots on the porch."

"Oh, cool," said Jonesy.

I narrowed my eyes.

She laughed. "Okay. Well, at least you can stand going on errands with your dad."

"What do you mean?" asked Maddie. "I love your father."

"I'm officially in high school, so he's officially in college mode," said Jonesy.

"We're freshmen," I said.

"We barely know our schedules," said Maddie.

Jonesy nodded. "I know! But my stupid cousin put off his college applications until it was too late and he didn't get in anywhere."

"Oh God, and you're an only child," said Maddie.

Jonesy nodded. "Exactly. Dad picked me up the first day of school with flyers for SAT prep!"

I even laughed at that.

Jonesy was super smart, especially in math. The reason she wasn't dealing with Mr. Pratt was because geometry was already behind her.

"He knows you're a genius, right?" said Maddie.

Jonesy just shook her head.

I laughed again. I hadn't done any high school work yet, and Jonesy was thinking about college.

"What's so funny?" asked Maddie.

I just shook my head. It would take too long to explain.

And then, just like that, it wasn't funny anymore. Just like that, I felt so irritated that I wanted to scream. I couldn't stand the chatter around me, the sun streaming into the cafeteria, or the sounds of chairs moving around.

I pushed my own chair back and stood, my food barely touched.

"I need to look at my English book before class," I said. "I forgot the quiz."

"Sure," said Maddie.

I tossed my tray on the conveyor line. The knives jangled.

I did grab my English book and go to class early, but I didn't open it. I sat there while everyone filed in after lunch. I passed up that quiz with another excuse about not bringing my book home.

The rest of the afternoon was unbearable. It was all I could do to stay. When the final bell rang, I closed my book and marched to the nearest exit sign. I didn't even stop at my locker. I just wanted out. Luke had some college-application activity like Model UN or the recycling club, so I had to walk home.

I hurried past the small groups of kids waiting for buses. I wished we lived in a bus zone so I could be whisked out of there in a smelly diesel way. I could just take one, anyway. But then someone might sit next to me. And I didn't want to talk to anyone.

Except Reagan. I wanted to talk with Reagan so bad it hurt.

Jesus, I thought. Your heart could have waited until we got through the first year of high school. You always said timing was everything. Well, you didn't time this very well.

I walked so fast I might as well have gone out for

cross-country. I tightened the straps on my new backpack—the one I'd picked out with Reagan because she insisted you couldn't take your middle school backpack to high school. I had stuffed her hoodie in it that morning. It was way too warm to have any chance of wearing it, but I needed something of hers along for the ride.

If you had just come with me, Reagan. If you had just come with me and bought a root beer and shared some chips, you could be making jokes about Señora Somebody and laughing at my luck to be paired with Nathan Hamill in biology. Yes, the Nathan Hamill who set the cafeteria on fire with his rocket experiment during the fifth-grade science fair. And yes, when he was getting supplies, I checked his backpack for matches.

I kicked a stone down the sidewalk. Then I kicked another one so hard I nearly lost my balance. It flew long and straight and rolled a house away. Too bad I hated soccer. I could be exercising and making new friends.

I almost tripped over the next stone. I caught my balance and stopped.

"Reagan," I said. "I need to talk to you!"

"I'm right here," Reagan said.

ME AND MY SHADOW

I looked around. I saw nothing except the sidewalk and the street and the fire hydrant. The only signs of humans were the shrieks of toddlers in a faraway backyard.

"You're not going to see me," said Reagan.

I shook my head. Fast. As much as I had thought about what Reagan would do and what Reagan would think in the last few weeks, I had never actually had an imaginary conversation with her. But this did not sound like imaginary Reagan.

I looked around again.

Maybe I had seen Reagan at the ball game.

I shook my head. This was nuts. There was no Reagan anymore. There was no Reagan at the game, and there was no Reagan here.

A breeze shook early yellow leaves off a nearby tree. An empty Starbucks cup rolled across the sidewalk, and dust blew into my eyes. I rubbed them, and my vision was blurred when I opened them again. A little Halloween music and I wouldn't have been surprised to see witches and goblins fly past.

But not Reagan. I shook my head again. I was hardly at my personal best, but I wasn't about to become some crazy lady talking to secret voices.

I kept walking home.

"It's really me," said Reagan.

I walked faster.

"Come on," Reagan said. "Give me a break."

I was obviously having delusions. Maybe this is what happened when you suddenly stopped exercising, like when you stopped taking some medications. I was having side effects like the ones listed in TV commercials.

So I started to jog. It felt good to run, and I picked up the pace.

"I HAVE A BUM HEART," yelled Reagan. "FOR GOD'S SAKE!"

That sounded way too much like Reagan to be a delusion. I slowed down.

"I can't get away too often, but you were having such a bad day," she said. "I feel so guilty."

"YOU feel guilty," I said. "YOU?"

"What do you mean?" asked Reagan.

"I left you there. At the gym."

"You told me to come with you," said Reagan.

"I should have made you."

"Like you could make me do anything," Reagan said.

"It would have been a good first time."

"Get over it. And seriously, SLOW DOWN."

I did. I slowed to a stroll.

"Better," said Reagan.

We walked like that for a couple of blocks. I felt normal for the first time since she had died.

"I actually thought I saw you at the baseball game."

"You know I hate baseball. All that waiting to get the ball into play."

"True."

"Besides, I'm not physical," said Reagan.

Sure, I thought. We kept walking.

"What's up with that geometry teacher?" asked Reagan. "He puts a new twist on getting your words in edgewise."

I laughed.

"And a burrito and chocolate milk? What was that? Kindergarten meets a food truck? Are you kidding me?"

"I panicked," I said.

"How did it taste?"

"Like I needed to find my blanket and take a nap."

We both laughed.

"I miss you," I said. "Really bad."

"I miss you, too," said Reagan. "We were going to have so much fun in high school."

"I couldn't even make myself go the first day."

"I know."

I shook my head.

"It has to get better," Reagan said.

"It won't. I'm not even sure I can drag myself back tomorrow."

"But you will," said Reagan.

We reached my door.

"I gotta go," said Reagan.

"Please don't," I said.

"No choice," she said.

I didn't reply.

"Say hi to your mom."

"Right," I said.

And then she was gone.

I stood on the steps for a few minutes, wondering if this was a "gotta go, see you later," or "gotta go, and who knows if I'll be back." Or "gotta go, and this whole thing was your brain melting down."

I grabbed my head. It didn't feel any different. It wasn't hot, and it wasn't vibrating like it was going to erupt.

I opened the door. Inside, Mom stood at the sink like Martha Stewart, with an apron wrapped around her skirt.

I didn't know she owned an apron.

My whole world, or what was left of it, was dissolving into the Twilight Zone.

"How was school, Sam?" asked Mom.

"What are you doing here?"

It was 3:30 p.m. She was supposed to be at work.

"Oh, I decided to finish up at home today," she said. "I'm making myself some tea and then I'll be back at the grindstone."

"Right," I said.

I put my backpack on the counter, and I opened the refrigerator door. I half expected to find Reagan looking back at me.

But I only saw cartons of milk and an army of yogurt.

"Want me to make you something?" asked Mom.

"What about that grindstone?" I asked.

"Sam," she said.

I grabbed a strawberry yogurt and leaned against the counter.

"I know you had a tough day," Mom said. "Do you want to talk about it?"

I shrugged.

"Did you see any of your friends?" she asked.

Reagan says hi, I thought.

I figured Maddie had talked to her mother, who talked to Mom, who rushed home from work. And put an apron over her suit. To make tea.

And they thought I was crazy.

I nodded. "I had lunch with Maddie and Jonesy."

"How did that go?"

"I'm guessing you already know," I said.

She stirred her tea.

"What about the grindstone?" I asked.

She pointed at my chair.

I sat.

"We're worried about you," she said. "Your father and I."

I nodded.

"We thought going back to school would help," she said.

"Mom, it's only been a week!" I said.

"Maddie did text her mom. Your friends are worried about you, too."

"Mom, there's nothing wrong with being upset about Reagan!" I said. "It's the freaking second week of school!!"

"Language," said Mom.

"She's dead, you know!"

For some crazy reason, Bradley's fart during Reagan's funeral came to mind. God. That was monumental. He had probably been working on an encore ever since. I started laughing. I couldn't stop.

"Sam!" said Mom. "What's so funny?"

I really couldn't stop laughing. Yogurt flew out of my nose.

Mom pulled her apron up and wiped bits of strawberry yogurt off the table.

And then I farted. That made me laugh even harder, and I couldn't stop.

I stood and walked away, laughing hysterically.

"Sam!" Mom called after me. "We need to talk!"

I laughed all the way upstairs. And when I shut my door and changed into sweatpants and a T-shirt, I lay down on my bed. For the first time in forever, my head hit the pillow without tears rolling down my cheeks.

ON THE ROAD AGAIN

When I woke the next morning, I stretched my arms over my head and yawned. I felt rested for the first time in weeks. I didn't even yell at Bradley when he barreled down the hall singing the Marines' Hymn.

And then I remembered talking with Reagan.

I figured it must have been a dream. And a good dream, too, not one of the ones I'd been having when we're playing ball or hanging out, and then I wake myself up because that couldn't happen because Reagan was dead.

But the more awake I became, the more I knew it wasn't a dream. It might have been impossible, but it wasn't a dream.

"Sam, sweetie," said Dad from outside my door. "Up and at 'em."

"Okay," I said. "I'm up."

That was new. Dad pounded on the door when we overslept. There were no "sweetie" calls. I sighed. Even though I was the cause, living in a house of eggshells was extremely annoying.

Luke parked in his usual next-galaxy parking space and sprinted for the school building to cram for the history quiz he just remembered. I walked slowly, listening for Reagan, avoiding incoming cars and boisterous groups of students to limit competing noises. I tightened my backpack strap so it stopped rustling.

But I had no pre-school visit. When I walked into Spanish, I wondered if I was going mad and would soon hear Reagan's voice with a foreign accent. Maybe not understanding anything said in that class had sent me off the deep end.

I looked for Maddie and Jonesy at lunch. No doubt, they would report my status again. If I didn't want the Martha Stewart treatment, I needed to be on my best behavior.

We sat at the same table—an unstable girl benefits from routine—and I dug into my macaroni and cheese salad. I still wasn't ready to make lunchtime selections myself, so I mimicked Jonesy no matter what she picked. I figured their reports on an improved appetite would be worth the price of unknown vegetables.

"I love that blouse!" said Maddie.

I wore the biology outfit. It even had the right pale yellow color in case macaroni and cheese flew onto it.

"Thanks!" I said.

I told myself not to talk about how Reagan liked it because it made her think of baby chicks. Today, I was a completely normal high school student.

"Feeling better?" Maddie asked.

I nodded. "Miles are covered one step at a time."

I closed my eyes. When did I start spouting lines from fortune cookies?

"That's so true," said Jonesy.

I wondered what best friend of hers died.

I looked around. I spotted a boy I didn't know. He was cute, with black cargo pants, a pale blue T-shirt, and longish straight hair. Time to act normal, I told myself.

I pointed. "Do you guys know him?"

"I didn't catch his name, but he's in my homeroom," said Maddie. "Cute, huh?"

"Definitely," I said.

"I'll get his name."

"He looks like this guy on my brother's travel team, but I don't think it's him," said Jonesy.

Maddie sighed. "That makes me think of Reagan," she said. "I can't imagine playing for the Blizzard without her."

"Maddie!" said Jonesy.

"That's okay," I said.

"Do you want to shoot around this weekend?" asked Maddie.

I shook my head.

"Too hard still?" asked Jonesy.

"Right," I said. I went back to my macaroni, hoping we could just focus on food.

"Well, you've got time before practice starts up again," said Jonesy.

I couldn't make my head nod. I put down my fork.

"I'm not playing," I said.

Maddie looked at Jonesy like I had lost my mind.

"What?" asked Jonesy. "Not play for the Blizzard?"

"Right," I said. I had no intention of playing for anyone again, but that was a start. "I'm going to concentrate on school."

"But without you and Reagan, we've got no front court!" said Maddie.

"Maddie!" said Jonesy.

"You guys were the team!" said Maddie.

"Maddie!" Jones said more loudly.

My face grew hot.

Maddie shut up.

"Basketball's not important now," said Jonesy. "Maddie?"

Maddie nodded. "Of course. You just surprised me."

So much for the low-key lunch conversation. We finished eating and headed to our lockers early, giving Maddie and Jonesy plenty of time to text the latest news to their mothers.

Sure enough, Mom was waiting for me when I walked through the back door. At least she wasn't wearing the apron. Yet.

"What's this I hear about you not playing basketball?" she asked.

"Are there any brownies left?" I asked.

"What brownies?" she said. "And wait, don't distract me. What's this about you not playing for the Blizzard?"

"I got confused," I said.

"What's confusing about basketball?"

"Confused about the brownies."

Mom looked confused.

"But that's okay," I said. "I'm not that hungry."

I headed for the stairs and my bedroom. I tossed my backpack on my chair. When did the simple act of going to school become so hard? And even when I had a game plan, I couldn't stick to it. And I couldn't blame Reagan for that. She might have been the creative one, but I was good at sticking to a game plan.

I lay on the bed and stared at the ceiling.

I needed to simplify things. I needed to get back to basics if I was going to survive. I needed to get back to putting one foot ahead of the other.

"You need a run," said Reagan.

"What?"

"Get off your butt and go for a run with me."

She was back! I hadn't been crazy. I pumped my fist.

"Yesterday I was walking too fast and now you want to run?" I asked.

"I haven't done anything all day," she said. "I'm ready."

What do you do all day when you do something? I wondered.

"Come on," said Reagan.

"Who put you in charge?" I asked.

"Come on," she said. "Better than talking to your dead friend in your room. Your mom thinks you have enough problems without that."

"I can't believe Maddie and Jonesy are posting reports about me," I said.

"They think they're helping," said Reagan.

"It's like having a personal NSA."

Reagan laughed.

"All right," I said. I changed into running shorts and a T-shirt and headed downstairs.

"Phone?" asked Reagan.

I rolled my eyes and retrieved my phone.

"Earbuds."

I turned around and grabbed them from my bureau.

When I walked into the kitchen, Mom looked up from the spreadsheets that covered the kitchen table. No apron, but a box of brownie mix sat on the counter and the oven was on preheat.

"Going for a run?" she asked.

"Thought it would do me some good."

That sounded so much better than telling her my dead best friend had been kind of bossy about it.

"Sounds great," she said. She pointed at the box. "We should have brownies when you get back."

"Thanks, Mom," I said.

Outside, I plugged the earbuds into my phone and jogged down the sidewalk. I sped up and sprinted for the mail truck at the end of the block.

"Who said anything about racing?" said Reagan, a little breathless. "Great way to pull a muscle."

I wasn't sure why a dead person would be concerned with muscle tears, but I didn't go there.

I slowed down and turned on the music.

It felt great to have Reagan running beside me again.

We ran at the same pace. Once, we checked and our legs were exactly the same length.

"So what's this about not playing for the Blizzard?" asked Reagan. "Jonesy almost stabbed herself with her fork."

"I'm not playing anymore," I said. "It wouldn't be the same without you."

"That means the Blizzard has no point guards, you know."

"I haven't played point in games for a while."

"Only because they had to play me somewhere," said Reagan.

"Right," I said.

"Well," said Reagan.

"Besides, the Blizzard still has Lilly Myers."

"I said point guards, not people who think they can play point."

"They'll figure something out," I said.

"What, someone new is going to show up?"

"You never know," I said.

"You love basketball," said Reagan. "I can't believe you're going to quit the Blizzard."

"I'm not playing high school basketball, either."

"That's ridiculous."

"Ridiculous was you dying," I said. Loudly.

The mailman looked at me.

God. I couldn't believe what I said.

Reagan didn't respond.

I slowed to a walk. "I'm so sorry, Reagan," I whispered. "I shouldn't have said that."

"It's not like I had any control," she said. "No one asked me if I'd rather die when I was ninety. Or fifty or thirty or even seventeen. I would have taken seventeen. Fourteen sucks."

"I'm sorry, Reagan," I said. "I didn't mean it."

I began to cry.

"Don't," said Reagan softly.

"I'm sorry," I said. "I wish it had been me instead of you."

"God, Sam. Don't say that. Trust me."

"Okay," I said. I wiped my nose on my T-shirt.

Reagan didn't say anything more for several minutes. I thought she may have left. I stopped when I reached Main Street.

"Feeling good enough for the duck pond?" asked Reagan.

"Sure," I said.

We retraced our steps and then turned for Elliot Park. We ran past the road to Grant and the gym where Reagan's heart exploded. She didn't say anything, but I sped up, not the smartest thing since I hadn't worked out since the day she died.

"Intervals?" asked Reagan. "Is that wise?"

"Not funny."

"You seem tense."

That seemed like a weird thing to come out of someone with experience in rigor mortis.

"Don't say whatever you are thinking," said Reagan.

"Don't you, like, know what I'm thinking?" I asked.

"I'm not some psychic from late-night TV."

I slowed down.

"Wow, you actually did what I said."

"Wait, we always did what you said!"

"You might be doing some revisionist history, isn't that what Mrs. Pettit in world history talked about during your first class?"

"Second class," I said. "But right. And since when did you sit in on my history class?" I asked.

"I have a lot of free time," Reagan said.

I didn't know how to respond.

"Just stay in shape. And you know, you might change your mind about basketball. And getting in shape at the last minute really sucks. Let's say I have intimate knowledge about the cardiovascular system."

"Will you run with me?" I asked.

Reagan didn't respond.

"Well?"

"I can only visit so often," Reagan said.

"Oh."

"So probably you shouldn't count on me for a running partner."

"Well, that's par for the course," I said. Reagan was not as dedicated to overall fitness as she was to basketball.

"I never missed a date for running," she said.

"It's the actual running part that I'm talking about."

"Yeah, well. You're supposed to listen to your body."

"Not your stomach," I said. "Sprinting for Dairy Queen doesn't count as running."

Reagan giggled. "I was going to install basketball hoops after I bought them. That way people could shoot baskets while they waited in line."

I nodded.

"That's off the table," she said.

"I'm sorry."

"Not as sorry as me."

We were silent for several seconds.

"Maybe I should start using Luke's weights. You were knocking me all over the place in pickup."

When we reached the park, we made one loop around the pond and headed back. There was a line of traffic at Broad Street, so we ran in place at the stop sign. Well, I did. I hadn't yet figured out the physical boundaries that Reagan had to respect. Look before you cross takes on a whole new meaning when you're hanging out with your dead best friend.

"Weights are a great idea," said Reagan. "We were going to start lifting after that class at the Y."

"So many things we were going to do."

"I know," said Reagan.

The cars moved on so we crossed the street. After another block, I slowed for the cooldown back to the house.

"Coming in?" I asked when we reached the steps.

"I can't," said Reagan.

"Chicken pot pie tonight!"

"I wish."

"Mom misses you," I said.

"I miss everyone," said Reagan.

And then she was gone.

I felt like the wind had been knocked out of me.

I sat on the steps, trying to pull it together. I took the ear-buds out and listened for Reagan's voice in case she returned for one last remark. I heard birds, barking dogs from blocks away, bus brakes from Broad Street, kids playing, and an overeager owl.

The world was all around me.

But I felt incredibly alone without Reagan.

HERE TODAY, GONE TOMORROW

I didn't hear from Reagan again for days. I walked home from school slowly like a cat tracking her prey, hoping to hear Reagan's voice. I started running every afternoon, but with my music turned so low that I couldn't tell what song was playing, in case she showed up. I talked to myself during my cooldowns, hoping that would prompt Dead Reagan to join me.

And then I started talking to imaginary Dead Reagan. But that didn't last because it was too hard to keep track of whether I was talking to imaginary Dead Reagan or real Dead Reagan.

Friday, I took the back entrance to Elliot's and walked home through the park, hoping the duck pond, or the pool, or the sledding hill, or the basketball courts would prompt Reagan to show up. But nothing.

At home, I changed to go running. But my legs felt sore, so I decided to lift weights instead. I put my phone on the garage counter and turned the music on high. I stretched on the mat Luke had borrowed from the Recreation Department, and

I grabbed a fifteen-pound dumbbell. I put one hand on the bench and started to do rows. The half hearts swung from my neck as I counted the reps from one to eight.

I did three sets of rows, and then I did twenty push-ups.

It was warm, so I opened the garage door.

I sat on the bench. The gray cat from across the street walked up the driveway and stared at me.

"What do you want?" I asked.

It hissed. That's what I got for feeding the stupid thing when our neighbors were on vacation.

"It never really liked you," said Reagan.

"I never really liked it," I said.

"You took care of it once for two whole weeks."

"And I got paid twenty dollars."

"Wait, you got paid for that?"

"Yes."

"But it was me that fed it half the time!"

"I didn't ask you to do that."

"Lord."

"Is that an expression, or is there someone else here I should know about?" I asked.

"Very funny."

"Not even an angel? I always wanted a guardian angel, you know, like Saint Michael."

"I am definitely not that. And he was an archangel."

"I'm not picky."

"I'll see if anyone's free."

Bradley burst through the door from the kitchen. "Can

you drive me to Tim's house?" He looked surprised. "Where's Mom? I thought you were talking to Mom."

"She hasn't come home yet," I said.

"Who were you talking to?" he asked.

"No one," I said.

He gave me his don't-lie-to-me look.

"Why don't you walk over to Tim's?" I asked. "It's okay with me."

He shook his head. "I need to take my telescope. It's too heavy to carry."

"Sorry," I said. "Why can't Tim come here?"

"Brand-new babysitter won't let him go anywhere."

"Sorry."

He shook his head. "Stop talking to yourself. It's mixing me up."

"I wasn't."

"Right," he said. He headed back inside.

"I should have asked if you could fly Bradley's telescope to Tim's," I told Reagan.

"I'm not a superhero," said Reagan. "I have no powers."

"Could have fooled me," I said.

"Speaking of flying, remember when we went to the circus and then we tried to rig up a flying-trapeze act off the garage roof?"

"I do," I said. "We were crazy."

"We were eight," said Reagan.

"The same year you won the Dribble Queen," I said.

"Hands down," said Reagan.

"Excuse me? I was a contender."

"Until I pulled out my between-the-legs move."

I had to agree. "First time I saw you do that."

"I practiced in my room."

I grabbed the kettle bell and did a set of squats, tired legs or not. I stretched my hamstrings, and then I did another set. I ended with standing bicep curls.

"Stick with it and you'll get really strong," said Reagan.

"That would be nice," I said.

I grabbed my sweatshirt from the folded Ping-Pong table.

"Gotta go," said Reagan.

"I miss you," I said.

"I miss you, too."

And then she was gone. And the wind rushed out of me. I sat down, barely able to breathe. The missing part was getting worse, not better.

Mom drove up, her car lights on for the fading afternoon sun. She grabbed her briefcase and walked into the garage.

I took a shallow breath. I tried to smile.

"I thought you were Luke," she said.

"Nope, it's me."

Mom reviewed the dumbbells on the floor and my sweat-band and workout clothes. "I didn't know you'd started to lift."

"Figured it wouldn't hurt," I said.

"Does this mean you're thinking about tryouts?" she asked. She smiled.

I shook my head.

"Oh," she said. "Well, it's the exercise that matters, right?"

I nodded. Even though I knew that wasn't what she was thinking at all. She was thinking, What can I do to get this kid back in the world again—playing ball, having fun?

And I was thinking how destroyed a person could feel when their dead friend leaves the room. It was like Reagan had died again.

Maybe it was all too hard to handle.

I fingered the half hearts. They always made me feel better. They were me and Reagan together. Like it was supposed to be.

At bedtime, when I put my head on my pillow, I still felt sad. I didn't cry, but it was more like my tears were frozen inside of me and couldn't come out.

———————————

Nathan Hamill stretched his arms and sent my pen flying to the floor. He leaned over and picked it up.

"Sorry," he said as he handed it to me.

I hadn't heard from Reagan in a week, and I wondered if the three visits were all I got, like the three wishes in *The Wizard of Oz* when Dorothy clicked her heels together. Or maybe she got one wish when she clicked her heels together three times.

Reagan would know, of course, because she paid attention to movies.

Nathan knocked his notebook onto the floor.

"Whoops," he said. And then he picked it up and put it in the same precarious place next to his elbow.

Nathan had been the most fidgety kid all through elementary school, and I couldn't believe I got stuck being partners with him. You wouldn't think it would matter so much in a lab, but ours had been experiment-free so far. The most action had been walking around the room to identify the safety equipment. I listened closely to the instructions for operating the fire extinguisher.

Ms. Dorothea clapped her hands. I wondered if that would make the lights brighter, but no, that meant the end to the most boring introduction to biology in world history. Not to be confused with world history, the class. Like peas and mashed potatoes, biology and world history should never mix.

"It's time for some fun," she said.

"I need fun," said Brain D. from the back.

Yes, he was also taking biology again. I wondered if he would ever leave high school.

"We're going to determine if yeast is alive!" she said.

Nathan snorted. "I'm not sure if she's alive or if we're watching a preprogrammed hologram."

I giggled. I didn't know he was funny.

"But first, we need to get organized," said Ms. Dorothea.

The class sighed. All we'd done so far was get organized. We'd been organizing for the year by learning scientific inquiry. And then we'd gotten organized for the actual subject by learning the principles of biological study. I wasn't sure I could take getting organized to do lab work. Although the idea of Nathan freelancing wasn't desirable, either.

"I need captains for each lab team," she said. "You'll

be responsible for maintaining your supplies, keeping labs on schedule, and posting your results."

The class buzzed at the possibility of doing experiments.

"Talk to your partner, and I want captain hands in a minute or so," said Ms. Dorothea.

Nathan nodded at me, like it was a done deal that I would be our captain.

But I didn't want to be in charge of anything.

I shook my head.

He looked surprised.

"I thought you'd want to be the captain," he said.

"Nope."

"You want *me* to be the captain?"

He pointed at his chest to make sure I understood.

"Sure," I said. I didn't want to be captain of anything. Not basketball teams, not school groups, not lab teams. I didn't want to talk to anyone if I didn't have to, never mind tell them what to do.

Except for Dead Reagan. Where was she?

"Okay," he said. He tentatively raised his hand.

I shifted into a more comfortable position on my stool.

I couldn't wait to figure out if yeast was alive.

After school, I changed into running clothes and headed for Elliot Park. I took a lap around the duck pond. On the turn behind the skate house, I spotted the Carlow High girls cross-country team heading up the sledding hill. Jonesy trailed a tight pack of runners.

I slowed down, not wanting any more invitations to

athletic teams. I was running because Dead Reagan convinced me it made sense.

Before she disappeared.

Maybe she knew that I was having trouble handling her coming and going. Maybe that made her decide to stay away. Although it seemed like that should be a joint decision. But then I remembered that she claimed she didn't know what I was thinking, which was odd because she always seemed to know what I was thinking when she was alive.

I circled the duck pond again and headed up the hill. I paid close attention to the stones that littered the ground and sucked wind until I was at the top at High Street. I stopped and leaned over to catch my breath. My running routes generally avoided the hill, and Reagan's routes always had us running down it.

It was amazing how fast you could lose your fitness. One minute you're racing down a court like you barely need oxygen, and the next minute you can't suck it in fast enough.

Or your heart stops, so there's no point to breathing.

I stood back up.

Maybe Dead Reagan wasn't reading my mind, and she was staying away because she didn't exist. Maybe Dead Reagan was all in my head. That was a lot more realistic than the possibility that I had run out of visits.

I jogged home, grabbed my laptop, and hit the Internet. I diagnosed my conversations with her as delusional behavior. I figured I could deal with some depression, but depression and delusions seemed a bit much.

Especially without Reagan to help.

From my online reading, I was most worried about having a psychotic depression, although maybe I really had the hallucinations that went with schizophrenia. There was something called paraphrenia, but you had to be old to get it. I wrote the term down for any future interest in vocabulary development. And while my geometry and history outfits were night and day, I really didn't think I was a candidate for a split personality.

I closed the laptop. Maybe I did need help. At least a psychologist could explain all these diseases to me.

Or maybe I needed to talk with Minister Morgan. He had been our pastor for a few years, and he seemed nice enough. He and his wife sponsored a youth group that Reagan dragged me to a couple times. And he was a professional who should be able to recognize the symptoms that required immediate psychiatric attention.

Or maybe I should start with Mr. Offerman.

But the idea of sharing Dead Reagan with anyone, even Dead Reagan the delusion, didn't sit well. Reagan was my best friend. I didn't get enough of her alive, and there wasn't that much of her to go around when she was dead.

I looked out the window to the street. I wondered if I would ever stop looking up the road, expecting to see Reagan sprinting around the corner to catch a ride to a game, or pedaling furiously on her bike and yelling for us to wait for her in driveway pickup.

I'd never stop looking. We'd have to move.

It had felt so good to run with her again last week, even

though running had never been my favorite activity.

Although now running was the only thing that made me feel better. Maybe it was because I could only think so much when I had to pay attention to my feet and the road and the traffic. Or maybe it was because when I was in motion, the world left me alone. My parents couldn't check up on me, my teammates couldn't guilt-trip me, and my schoolbooks couldn't glare at me from the desk in my bedroom.

When I was running, I almost felt alive again. Maybe not as kicking alive as the yeast we'd deemed to be among the living that morning, but alive.

Unlike Reagan.

A little gust knocked sidewalk leaves into the air. Dark clouds moved across the sky.

I fingered the half hearts and prayed that Reagan would visit me again.

HALF HEART IN A HAYSTACK

Mr. Pratt said something about angle-sliding angels. I sat back in my chair and settled in for another round of What Did He Really Say? His whiteboard writing was horrible, too. He did fine with lines and rays, but his letters looked like marker mumbles. Most students coped by watching geometry videos on YouTube. They posted them at night with the hashtag #notpratt.

I yawned and reached for the half hearts around my neck. I found nothing. No chain. No half hearts.

I attacked my throat, groping for the silver chain. Nothing.

I reached halfway down my shirt and to the bottom of my bra.

Still nothing.

Mr. Pratt looked at me strangely.

I smiled back like don't most girls adjust their bras during geometry? But I was in full panic mode.

I took a long breath to calm down. I needed to think.

I knew I had it on after I dressed that morning because I'd looked in the mirror and the light bounced off one half heart. I'd wondered if it was mine or Reagan's.

It must have come off in the shower after gym class that morning. I had my weekly gym class at 7:00 a.m.

But no. We were late coming in from playing soccer. And since I overslept and missed breakfast, I had scrambled to change and make it to the vending machine for chips and choc-olate milk before class. I didn't take a shower. The half hearts didn't go down the drain. And I had them before we played soccer because I had stood in the locker room, twirling them, before Maddie took my arm and herded me outside.

I ran my finger around my neck again. Still nothing.

Stupid soccer. Stupid sport. My half heart—and Reagan's half heart—had fallen off on the stupid soccer field. Where they were hidden in a million blades of grass. Not on a civilized basketball court where if you lost an earring or a contact, you stopped play and searched until you found it.

I had no idea how to search a soccer field.

"Ms. Wilson?" said Mr. Pratt. "Are you with us today?"

"Sorry," I said.

"So?" he said. "Would you like to answer my question at the board?"

"No," I said. "I wouldn't."

Mr. Pratt looked surprised. "Okay," he said. "Anyone else?"

I felt like crying. I didn't know what I would do without Reagan's half heart around my neck. The part of Reagan that stayed with me every minute of every day. That I grabbed whenever I felt lonely or scared.

No. No. No.

I ran from world history to the soccer field when the final bell rang.

I stood at midfield. Looking at those million blades of grass, I was crushed. There was no way I was going to find the half hearts. But I took a deep breath and tried to remember the gym class. Coach Gray treated us like we were a team and not phys ed students. She made us take shooting practice against the goal closest to the woods. Then we played and Coach Gray put me at midfielder.

I had run all over the place. Great. Finding the half hearts would be impossible.

I jogged to the goal near the woods, feeling worse than the full gray skies threatening to open up. And I walked around its penalty area for half an hour, hoping to see a glint of silver. I searched until the skies let loose with a downpour. I ran back to the building, soaked, and headed back to my abandoned world history book.

On the way, I saw Goth Boy sitting by himself in Mr. Pratt's classroom, drawing in his notebook.

I stopped. Water dripped from my clothes.

I blushed when he noticed me.

"What are you looking for?" he asked.

"What?"

"I saw you," he said. He pointed at the window. "Earring?"

I had never heard Goth Boy speak. And now he was giving speeches about my personal business.

"Why are you here?" I asked.

"Not answering questions in class," he said. "I have detention for insubordination."

"You're kidding."

"Nope. Mr. Pratt thinks if I sit here for a week, I'll change my mind." He laughed. "I won't."

"I didn't answer a question today," I said.

"I know," he said. "I'm in your class."

I shot him a look. "So why didn't Pratt make me stay?"

"I've got a dead attitude. You've got a dead friend."

My face flushed. "Nice," I said.

What a jerk. I marched to the history classroom and grabbed my book.

I texted "When done?" to Luke.

He texted back "4."

I ran through the rain to his truck and I waited, dripping again, glad that I had nagged him until he gave me the extra key.

I walked to school early the next morning and completed my tour of the penalty area at the soccer field. The grass was still wet from yesterday's rain, and my shoes were soaked by the time the first bell rang. I searched again the rest of the week, glad that early gym class only happened on Mondays. The soccer teams had practice after school, so I only had the mornings to look for the half hearts.

By the time I ran to Spanish on Friday morning, I'd found

barrettes, paper clips, quarters, pennies, pens, three whistles, and five keys. But no silver chain and no half hearts.

I told myself there was hope as long as I kept looking. During geometry, I stared out the window at the field, taking some comfort in knowing that the half hearts were on it. But then I felt bad because Reagan hated soccer more than I did. And now her half heart might be stuck out there forever. I wondered if she knew and that's why she had stayed away—I couldn't even take care of the heart she'd left behind.

The bell rang, and we pushed back our chairs. Another hour of my life wasted.

"Samantha," said Goth Boy, still sitting at his desk.

Maybe Mr. Pratt had glued him to it.

"I have a metal detector," he said. "That's your only option."

"What?"

Kids rushed past me to the hall and their next class.

"I figure it must be jewelry."

"How do you know I'm still looking?"

He pointed to the window. "Saw you walking off the field before school."

I shrugged.

"Meet me there at nine tomorrow morning and I'll bring it."

I looked at him like he was out of his mind.

"It's your only hope."

I didn't like him. But he was probably right. And I was desperate.

"Okay."

The next morning, I rode my bike to the soccer field. Goth Boy was already there, fiddling with the control of his metal detector. He was dressed normally, with khaki shorts and a faded yellow golf shirt.

"Hi," I said, wondering if the school guard was on site on Saturdays.

"What are we looking for?" he asked.

I showed him my eighth-grade picture on my phone. "That," I said, pointing to the necklace. "With two halves instead of one."

He nodded.

"It's sterling silver," I said.

Goth Boy smiled. He tapped the metal detector. "This thing will find a trace of metal," he said. "Ready?"

We walked onto the field, which was covered in dew. Goth Boy methodically walked with the metal detector in the penalty area near the woods, headphones in place. He walked back and forth, overlapping his tracks, stopping periodically to grab pennies and bottle caps from the grass. I walked beside him, staring intently at the ground, hoping that the morning sun would shine on the half hearts in the grass.

I couldn't believe I had been so careless. Reagan was always good with her half heart, usually storing it in the zipped pocket in her backpack before practice or games, always asking Mom to keep it when she took us to the pool. She took care of the important things. She always took care of us. I was just along for the ride.

I felt bad. So bad that my eyes welled up and the tears started. I turned away from Goth Boy so he couldn't see me. Then I really started crying. I stepped away, and my shoulders heaved up and down. I yelped.

"Hey, you okay?" asked Goth Boy.

I nodded. Get your act together, I told myself. Get tough this very second. I made myself breathe long and deep.

"Fall allergies," I said. I cleared my throat. "All this grass. A million blades of allergy."

"Good thing you play basketball and not soccer," he said.

Weird. I never told him I played basketball.

"I've never liked soccer," I said.

"Me neither," said Goth Boy. "Come on, I'll show you how this works." He hesitated. "My name is Kevin, by the way."

I blushed. He knew I didn't even know his name.

He shrugged. But then he smiled.

We walked the far side penalty area again, and this time I held the metal detector and found a bunch of quarters, three old metal cleats, another whistle, and a 1962 dime. The metal detector display showed you the intensity of the signal. You could tune it if you wanted to focus on the high-end ones. We gave up on the penalty area, and we spent the next hour searching the outer edges of the field.

A 1937 nickel, two keys, three ball bearings, and a Titleist golf ball later, and Kevin stopped walking.

"Sorry, I have to go now," he said. "I told my mom I'd help her take some stuff to Goodwill before lunch."

I was disappointed, but I hadn't expected a miracle.

Kevin pulled the golf ball out of his pocket. "You want this?"

I shook my head.

"I'm sorry we didn't find your necklace," said Kevin. "But we can try again."

"I felt like I was on an archaeological dig," I said.

Kevin laughed. "I do like old stuff."

"I had you figured for a *Star Trek* kind of guy," I said.

Kevin laughed again. "But some of those spaceships come from ancient galaxies."

He stuck his detector over his shoulder, and we walked down the path to the bike stand. Halfway there, he put out his arm to stop me. Then he leaned over and picked something up.

He held out my silver chain with both half hearts still attached.

I grabbed it and clenched it tight. "Thank you so much!"

He smiled.

"I can't believe you found it."

Kevin smiled more broadly.

I took a deep breath. I fingered the half hearts, still not believing I had them.

"One heart belonged to my friend Reagan," I said.

He nodded.

"It's dumb, I know," I blurted. "My brother Luke bought it for his first girlfriend and then she broke up with him before he even got them engraved. So he gave them to me. And Reagan and I have been wearing our half hearts since we were ten."

I hesitated. "Wore our half hearts."

Kevin didn't know what to say.

I let out a long breath. I felt so stupid unloading to Goth Boy.

"It's nice," he finally said. He stared at the half hearts in my hand. His eyes widened. "Oh geez, and . . ."

I narrowed my eyes at his face that said how ironic that Reagan died from a busted heart.

"Nothing," he said.

"Good," I said. I didn't need some goth boy lecturing me on symbolism.

"You might check the clasp," Kevin said. "A jeweler can put a better one on if it's broken."

"I will," I said. "And look, I'm sorry we wasted so much time on the field."

"No problem," said Kevin. "This is my hobby. And now we have cleats from the last century."

"I owe you," I said.

"I'm just glad we found it."

"Thanks again," I said.

"No problem," he said.

Kevin pulled out his bike and rode away. But when he reached the parking lot, he turned to me and grinned.

I waved. And I watched him pedal away.

"That's so sweet," said Reagan.

"Shut up," I said.

"He's such a nice boy."

"I am so embarrassed," I said.

"What? That my heart was on the side of the road?"

"Yes. After Kevin spent two hours searching the field."

"Now Goth Boy is Kevin?"

"Shut up."

"I think he likes you. And you thought he was weird."

"He is," I said. "But that's okay."

"Are you going to the wild side?"

I shrugged.

"Oh God. Please don't put pink highlights in your hair."

"I could use a change," I said.

"Don't go crazy on me. And please don't take me on any more soccer fields," Reagan said.

"Turns out I didn't leave you on a soccer field."

"You think leaving me on the side of the road is any better?"

I smiled. "I'll be more careful."

"You better."

I walked my bike home, feeling like a different person.

I checked the half hearts a hundred times before I reached the house.

DRIVING THE POINT HOME

"Here," said Brain D. in geometry class. He waited until Mr. Pratt turned to the board and handed me a note.

It was from Kevin.

Want to hit some golf balls with me?

If you'd asked me what question I'd least expect from this goth boy decked out in a black turtleneck and black chinos sporting new purple streaks in his dyed black hair and engaged in an all-out war on the math faculty about the role of classroom participation in American education, it would be whether I would like to hit golf balls with him.

I looked at Kevin. He grinned.

He'd told me that his dad worked at the country club when he wasn't teaching at Carlow Community, but I didn't translate that into the golfing aspects.

I smiled back. I ripped a page from my notebook.

But I don't play golf.

I handed the page to Kevin when Mr. Pratt turned his back to write on the board.

But Kevin didn't respond for the rest of class. I sat there, paying less attention to Pratt than usual, wondering if I had misjudged Kevin and he really was a disenfranchised loner who had catastrophic designs on the school. Or maybe he was schizophrenic or had some really bizarre mental illness and I should stay away. He didn't seem to have any friends.

Of course, neither did I. And when Maddie and Jonesy found out I wasn't going to play high school basketball, either, I would probably lose my lunch group, too. Unless they were being paid to be spies on my mental health.

I zoned out so much that I only realized the bell had rung when everyone pushed back their chairs. I gathered my things and momentarily forgot my next class. I hurried into the hall and tried to remember who I followed from geometry to my next educational adventure.

"So?" Kevin stood beside me.

"Oh," I said. "I don't play golf."

"I can read," he said.

"And be sarcastic," I replied.

"I'll teach you," said Kevin.

"To be sarcastic?" I asked.

He rolled his eyes. "Good one." He hesitated. "I mean golf."

"Where?"

"Country club range," he said. "My dad's the pro."

Oh. The psychiatric ward in my head morphed into lavish fairways and a cute putting green.

"Or there's a range at the edge of town. Sometimes I go there. It's kind of funky." He hesitated. "But that means riding bikes with a few clubs, and that doesn't make sense if we can practice for free at the country club."

"Is that why you're so good riding with a metal detector?" I asked.

Kevin laughed. "Maybe."

"But I really don't play," I said. "Except for mini golf in the summer."

"Are you any good?" Kevin asked.

"Killer with lighthouse holes."

"Then come and I'll show you how to swing the other clubs."

I shook my head. "I didn't picture you as a golfer."

He shrugged. "Kind of a family thing."

"Okay," I said. "When?"

"How about Saturday?" he asked. "Like around ten?"

"I'll see if my dad can drop me off."

Mr. Pratt came to the doorway and glared at us.

"Oh, crap," said Kevin. The hall was nearly deserted. "We better get moving."

I just stood there, trying to remember my next class.

"I think you go to biology," said Kevin.

"Right," I said. And I jogged down to room 212, wondering why Kevin knew my schedule. And wondering more why I couldn't seem to remember it.

Mom put scrambled egg whites, whole wheat toast, and turkey bacon on the table.

"Look, I threw out all your cereal boxes, except for the Cheerios. They have way too much sugar and I'm not raising diabetics," she said.

"Can we still put sugar on our Cheerios?" asked Bradley.

"No," she said.

"Couldn't this wait until I go to college next year?" said Luke.

"No," said Mom. "It's a done deal. It may be too late for you, but I can help the others."

"That's not fair," said Bradley. "Then Luke gets twice as many years of good cereals as me!"

"Nice numbers for someone who puts off his math homework until the last minute," said Mom. "Now eat."

"Can I have an instant breakfast?" I asked. "That's nutritional. And I'm not hungry."

Mom shook her head. "I'd rather you eat some eggs."

"Please?"

"Okay," she said. "Last time. We're not buying any more of that stuff."

I nodded and headed for the pantry.

"Can I have an instant breakfast, too?" asked Bradley.

"No," said Mom.

"But that's not fair," said Bradley.

"Life's not fair, son," said Dad, putting a half-eaten slice of pretend bacon back on his plate. He was dressed in his weekend garb of jeans and Bruce Springsteen concert T-shirt.

"Come on," he told me. "I'll drop you off at the library now."

I nodded. I did ask to go to the library. And I did need to go to the library. Eventually.

We headed out and took a right on Broad Street.

"Dad, I changed my mind about the library, but anyway, this isn't the way."

"I know," said Dad.

A few minutes later, he pulled into Polly's, where we sat in the car and ate double chocolate and cinnamon donuts. It's amazing how hungry I got once I opened the donut bag.

When we finished, Dad turned the key in the starter. "Okay, where to?" he asked.

"The country club."

"Say what?"

"The driving range at the country club. I'm going to hit balls with this guy from school."

"That's some change of mind!"

"I didn't want Mom to know," I said.

"She is your mother," said Dad.

"I know, but I don't want to get her all excited that I'm, like, normal."

"Because you have a date?" asked Dad.

"It's not a date!" I said.

"Who's the guy?"

"Kevin. I don't know his last name."

"I'm supposed to drop you off with some guy Kevin who doesn't have a last name?"

It didn't seem the time to tell him that I'd met Kevin last weekend at the soccer field without knowing his first name.

"At the golf course where his father is the pro or something."

"Tom Holt?" Dad asked. "He was a couple years behind me in school."

"Maybe," I said. "So let's say the guy is Kevin Holt. That sounds right."

"Shouldn't you know from class?"

"He doesn't talk much," I said.

Dad gave me a concerned look and then turned back to the road.

"Okay," he said. "Do you have your phone with you?"

"Yes. And I will text you at the first sign of trouble." I paused. "Right after I call 911."

"Please do."

Dad drove out to the country club. He headed for the driving range. On the wide practice tee, equally spaced golfers swung at 50-, 100-, 150-, and 200-yard markers out on the range. Their golf bags sat straight up in green metal stands, guarding buckets of balls.

Kevin leaned against the small concession hut. He wore black jeans and a Superman T-shirt. And black golf shoes.

"That's the guy?" asked Dad as he pulled next to the hut.

"Yup," I said.

"If he didn't have the shoes on, I wouldn't have guessed he had anything to do with golf," Dad said.

I got out of the car and shut the door.

"Call when you need a ride," Dad said.

I nodded.

Dad gave Kevin a wave, and Kevin returned it.

"You ready?" asked Kevin.

"Teach me that," I said, pointing to a golfer who slammed his drive to the farthest reaches of the range.

Kevin laughed. "He's like a two-handicapper."

"Oh," I said. "I take it I would be a sky-high-handicapper?"

"I don't think you're handicapped at all," he said.

I smiled.

For someone who didn't want to discuss the Pythagorean theorem publicly, Kevin blew me away with how he could break down the angles of a golf swing. Well, the parts of a golf swing you use to hit a borrowed seven-iron.

"Follow through," said Kevin. "You follow through on every shot, from your driver through your putter."

He poked another range ball into place with the head of his wedge, and I stood over it with my borrowed club. I swung again, thinking about my follow-through. I muffed it, hitting nothing but air.

"Crap," I said.

Kevin laughed. "But that was a nice follow-through."

"Very funny." I reached for another ball. I took a deep breath. And I relaxed everything like I did at the free-throw line. I took the club back and hit the ball and followed through. The ball took off in a nice arc, right for the 100-yard sign, and banged it.

"Whoa!" said Kevin.

"Is there a prize for that?" I asked.

Kevin laughed. And then he pushed another range ball toward me.

Hitting the sign was all the motivation I needed. My goal was another big bang. I hit half a bucket of balls under Kevin's supervision, setting up, lining my shot to the target, taking the club back slowly, and following through. It did remind me of the free-throw line, one of the few times on a basketball court that you are totally in control. I liked the repetition, and I liked the focus. I nearly forgot that Kevin was a few feet away.

"You're like a machine," Kevin said.

"What?"

"You really concentrate," he said.

"Oh, thanks." I rested the club against my hip.

"And you are really athletic."

I shrugged.

"I know you're a great basketball player," he said. "But, wow, you could be a great golfer, too."

I was a great basketball player, I thought. But then, all of a sudden, my mood turned dark as I remembered my last time playing basketball with Reagan at Grant gym. Her tumbling into me twice, her bumping me as she guarded me closely, and her shoes squeaking as she pivoted one way and the other to set up a play.

God, Reagan loved the sound of squeaking sneakers. She was so obsessed with it that we twice snuck into gyms that had just been refinished because those floors squeaked the best.

"Sam?"

Reagan could simply not be dead. Some nightmare had slammed into my real life and stuck to me. Those sneakers were still squeaking somewhere I couldn't find.

"Sam, you look terrible," said Kevin. "Are you okay?"

I dropped the seven-iron. Kevin picked it up and handed it back to me.

I shook my head. "Listen, thanks and everything, but I need to go."

"What?"

"I need to go."

"Um, okay." He put the club back in his bag. "Is your dad picking you up?"

I nodded. "Now."

"Okay," said Kevin.

"I'm supposed to meet him at the entrance," I said. "He's really busy."

"Did I do something wrong?" asked Kevin.

"What?"

"Did I say something wrong?" asked Kevin.

"Oh, no," I said. "I just lost track of time."

Right. I just lost track of reality. I walked away, and when I reached the club house road, I ran all the way to the entrance. Then I walked toward town, past the soccer fields and the mall.

I walked faster and faster. I didn't know what was wrong

with me. Every time I thought things were getting easier and I started to feel like the old Sam, I got blown off course by a vivid memory of Reagan that seemed more real than my life. Dead Reagan helped, but she couldn't play one-on-one or ride bikes or do a soft shoe on a newly refinished, squeaky basketball floor.

It took me an hour to get back to town. I walked past the side entrance to Elliot Park, and then I turned around and took its path. I walked to the pool, now drained of its water. I stood at the fence and looked at the pile of leaves collected in the deep end.

A skinny boy bounced a ball at the nearby basketball court and occasionally threw up shots that smacked against the backboard. I sank to the ground and sat cross-legged. I watched a leaf drift down inside the pool, knocking against the side in rhythm with the bouncing ball. Finally, it reached the bottom.

It felt like the life had been drained out of me. I closed my eyes, and I focused on breathing in and out. It was cold, and I tucked my arms around me. I pushed everything out of my head except the bouncing ball. Three bounces, and then a clang from the rim or a smack against the worn backboard. Three more bounces, and another clang or another smack. Again and again and again.

It would not go away. Apparently the kid would never make a basket.

Bounce. Bounce. Bounce. Clang.

I tried breathing deeper. I needed to get everything out of my head. I needed a few minutes of peace.

Bounce. Bounce. Bounce. Smack.

And then my brain kicked in Reagan's standing dribble. Bounce, two, three. Bounce, two, three. Hearing that ball bounce in my head like that got me through waltzing in seventh-grade gym class.

"Come on," Reagan said softly. "You'll catch a chill."

"I hit the hundred-yard marker," I said.

"I saw that."

"Kevin thinks I'm crazy."

"You are crazy if you think shivering in this cold is smart."

"Thanks."

"Let's get you home."

I nodded.

"Come on."

I got to my feet slowly.

Dead Reagan and I walked home from the pool that had no water and the kid who couldn't shoot straight.

UNAVOIDABLE

It's hard to avoid someone sitting next to you in geometry.

"You okay?" asked the boy who didn't talk in class on Monday morning.

Brain D. poked the kid in front of him. "Goth Boy doth speak," he said.

I pretended I didn't hear Kevin or Brain D. I fiddled with my geometry textbook, turning pages like I was looking for Extreme Inspiration.

"Okay?" asked Kevin again.

Unless I had suddenly lost my hearing or could do a good impression of the said hearing loss, I was screwed.

"I'm okay," I said.

Kevin nodded. He started to say something else, but Mr. Pratt walked into the room. Kevin bit his lip as soon as he saw the man. He really hated him.

But I was off the hook.

Mr. Pratt started on the interior ages of pollywogs, and I

found the right place in the book. It was inspirational because the text was clearly enunciated with solid type and articulate spelling and I understood the interior angles of polygons right away. Geometry wasn't that bad. I really needed to do some homework.

I glanced at Kevin. Still half biting his lip, he stared fiercely at the whiteboard. I got the feeling he knew what Mr. Pratt was talking about without looking at his book.

When the bell rang, I raced out before Kevin could try talking to me again.

But he did find me at lunch.

"Hi," he said.

Maddie and Jonesy beamed excited looks back and forth like they were sending mission-critical Morse code.

"Hi," I said.

"I didn't write down some stuff from geometry today," he said. "Can I get the notes from you after school?"

Nice, I thought. "Sure," I said. "Find me here?"

"Excellent," he said. "And thanks."

As soon as he was out of earshot range, Maddie and Jonesy fell over themselves asking about Kevin.

"That's Goth Boy?" asked Maddie. "Him?"

I nodded.

"He's so cute you barely notice the black," said Jonesy.

"His socks were purple," said Maddie. "Dark purple but purple."

"You notice people's socks?" I said.

"I see the entire ensemble," said Maddie.

"What's the deal with this guy?" asked Jonesy.

"He wants my geometry notes," I said. "You heard him."

"Right," said Jonesy.

"Your notes," said Maddie. She winked.

After closing my locker, I thought of reasons to explain to Kevin why I forgot about meeting him for the notes. With my non-existent after-school activities, the best I could do was early onset dementia. So, of course, I bumped into him coming out of the first-floor hall.

"Me again," said Kevin.

"I see that," I replied.

We kept walking, and I stopped once we reached the cafeteria tables.

I pulled my backpack off my shoulder. "Let me get those notes."

Kevin smiled. "I don't need your notes," he said. "I just wanted to talk to you."

I felt stupid. I rezipped the backpack.

"Walking home?" he asked.

I nodded.

"Can I come with you?"

I shrugged.

Kevin took that as a yes.

We walked past the bus kids and the line of cars heading out of the parking lot. I glanced at Luke's distant truck. I fingered the extra key in my jacket pocket. I wished I knew how to drive.

We walked silently for several minutes. When we reached the stop sign at Broad Street, Kevin cleared his throat. "So," he said.

He played with the zipper on his jacket. "So I really didn't make you mad on Saturday?"

"No, I had to go," I said.

"You practically ran away," Kevin said.

I shrugged.

"I shouldn't have brought up basketball," he said. "But it struck me that you were so athletic, you know?"

"Lots of girls are athletic." Surely he'd heard of Title IX.

"Oh, of course!" he said. "I mean, sure."

I looked at him.

"It was cool," he said. "You learned to swing a club so quickly."

I shrugged.

He laughed. "Dad spends whole summers getting clients to that point."

"I did hit the hundred-yard sign," I said.

He laughed. "You dented it."

We had reached my driveway. I stopped.

"Your house?" Kevin asked.

"Yes."

Bradley charged out of the front door, followed by his buddy Tim. Holding water guns, they ran up the sidewalk.

"Aliens," I said. "They come and go."

Kevin chuckled. "I wish I had some aliens at my house," he said. "There's just me and my parents."

"Sounds nice and quiet," I said.

He shrugged. "If you like swimming in a fishbowl."

"Well," I said, "I better get inside. Homework and all that."

Like I did mine.

"Sure," said Kevin.

"Bye," I said. Kevin walked away.

I headed to the steps.

"Hey!" Kevin called.

I turned.

"Mini golf?" he said. "Saturday? Even the playing field?"

"Um, okay," I said. "I mean if I'm free. Let me check my schedule and get back to you."

"Cool." Kevin grinned.

"Bye," I called.

I swung open the kitchen door to find Luke eating a sandwich at the kitchen table.

"Thanks for the ride," I said.

He shrugged. "Recycling club got called off. Some freshman forgot the collection bags."

I grabbed a few of his potato chips. "Wasn't there something else for you to do? Sing Earth Day songs or something?"

"Very funny. Besides, I found you on the way home, but you were so engrossed talking with Goth Boy that you didn't see me."

I blushed.

Luke pointed at me. "Woo! She likes him!"

"He's just a guy in geometry," I said. "We hit some golf balls Saturday."

"Already had the first date!" he said.

"Not a date," I said.

"Right."

He grinned and took another bite of his sandwich.

EVERYBODY KNOWS REAGAN

The doorbell rang.

Luke and Bradley nearly killed each other rushing to answer it. Luke could act like a ten-year-old in a heartbeat.

Bradley powered back into the kitchen.

"Boy in Black to see Samantha," he said into his hands like it was a megaphone. "Boy in Black to see Sam."

"Stop," said Mom. "Luke?"

"What he said," called Luke from the hall.

He ushered a red-faced Kevin into the kitchen. Indeed, he was at his Goth-Boy finest, with black jeans, black polo short, and black Converse. A black baseball cap covered the streak of purple in his hair.

"Hi, Kevin," I said.

He waved.

"Have a gluten-free muffin," said Mom.

He shook his head. "Thanks, but I already had breakfast."

"Oh, take one for the road," said Dad. "Please."

"Dad," I said.

I swigged the last of my milk and stood. "We have to go."

"Early tee time at the mini-golf course?" asked Dad.

"Very funny," I said.

"Mini golf?" said Bradley. "Really? Can I come?"

"No," I said.

Bradley stuck out his lower lip.

"I'll take you soon," said Dad. He put his arm around Mom, who was so happy to see me making new friends that she ignored all the remarks about her muffins.

And to be honest, I felt more normal than I had for a long time.

"Bye," I said. I grabbed Kevin's arm and whisked him outside.

"They seem nice," he said.

"Uh-huh."

Kevin's bike lay on the sidewalk.

"Let me run into the garage and get mine."

We rode down Broad and over to Fruit Street and then out Dairy Road to this nine-hole mini-golf course and driving range that a local farmer had built next to his grazing fields and green-and-white silo. A tall mesh fence kept the cows safe from hooks and slices. A red shack guarded the gate to the course.

We were early for the 10:00 a.m. opening. We laid our bikes next to the sign stuck in the ground that said "Closes Oct 15 for season."

I pointed at it. "Unless it snows earlier."

"Ah, come on," said Kevin. "Nothing more fun than playing mini golf on a snow-covered carpet."

"Don't tell me you're one of those nuts who plays golf in the snow," I said. "I've seen you people—knocking around in your parkas and boots looking for neon-green golf balls."

"Don't forget snowshoes for the deep stuff," he said.

"God," I said.

"Mini golf is great practice for icy greens."

I laughed. Kevin was funny. If he talked in class, it would make geometry tolerable.

Kevin pulled out his notebook. "Hey, you mind if I sketch this fast?" He pointed at the silo.

"Sure," I said.

He quickly drew the silo and the little stand of white birches beside it.

"You're good," I said.

"I want to be an artist," he said.

"You are an artist."

He grinned.

A teenage girl drove a golf cart over from the farmhouse, rolling up and down a hilly pasture on the way. She pulled within a foot of us and shut off the motor.

"You guys are eager," she said.

"Early worm gets the birdie," said Kevin.

I chuckled.

The girl gave him a blank look.

Kevin grinned.

The girl shook her head and opened the gate to the course.

"Crazy people get the first round free," she announced.

"Thanks," said Kevin. "Now, is a round nine or eighteen holes?"

"You didn't just ask that," she said.

Kevin handed her money for the second nine, and she opened the red shack, raised the window, and handed change back. Next, she handed Kevin two golf balls.

"Have fun," she said. "Pick out your putter from the rack near the first tee."

After five holes, Kevin and I were tied. I had well-tuned skills from years of summer-vacation mini golf at the coast. Each year, we stayed at the Golf View cottage across from the Beach Ball Adventure Golf course.

I expertly rolled the ball through a windmill into the cup for a hole in one on the sixth hole.

"You realize I was the putting champion at junior golf camp for three years running," Kevin said.

"You have three holes left to prove it," I said.

"Oh, this is a nine-hole match?" he said. "You don't think beginner's luck can last the full eighteen holes?"

He had no idea of the intensity of the Reagan and Sam Beach Ball Adventure Golf tournaments. Reagan always came with us on summer vacations. We would play a practice round in the mornings before heading to the beach for body surfing. Then we played an official tournament each afternoon. The Golf View cottage came with free passes. On the final afternoon, we played thirty-six holes for the Ultimate Final Championship.

Kevin made his putt, too.

When we took the two steps to the seventh tee, I stopped short. I didn't remember who won the Ultimate Final Championship last July. The summer had become a blur. We'd gone on vacation after July 4 and before basketball camp. I remembered the exceptionally big waves for Maine the first few days because of a storm at sea, and I remembered playing cards and eating popcorn the day it rained. But I couldn't remember playing the Ultimate Final Championship with Reagan.

"Sam?" asked Kevin.

I didn't understand how I could I forget that.

"I'm okay, just trying to remember something," I said.

"What's so important that it's keeping you from the seventh hole?"

I smiled. "Come on, I have work to do."

We both suffered from lapses of concentration on seven and eight and made two-putt pars. That was inexcusable given our obvious talents.

We looked over the ninth hole—the signature hole of the course. You had to play the ball around a miniature silo in the middle by banking your ball off a horse trough on the left or a chicken coop on the right. And you had to time your putt so it entered a swinging fence when it swung open and hit the hole in the center of a corral.

"Is there a famous mini-golf course builder?" I asked.

"Like the equivalent of Jack Nicklaus or Pete Dye?"

"Impressive. You know golf course designers."

"Only from reading *Sports Illustrated*. Turns out there's all kinds of junk in there."

"Besides basketball, you mean," Kevin said.

"Saying I have a one-track mind?" I asked.

"No," said Kevin.

"Good, because I'll have you know I read articles about college and pro basketball, women's and men's."

"A real Renaissance woman."

I stuck my tongue out, and then I stepped forward and planned my putt.

I took a measured breath. Then I smacked the ball off the coop and through the open gate into the hole in the corral. The ball hit the cup a bit hard and spun around a few times. But it stayed in.

"Outstanding," said Kevin.

He putted off the chicken coop, too. His ball barely made it through the gate. It caught the left edge of the cup, but it spun away.

"I win the side," I yelled. "I win the side!"

"You did," said Kevin, grinning.

"I'll take a Diet Coke," I said, pointing to the drink machine next to the shack.

Kevin looked at me curiously. Whoops. I had slipped into Sam-and-Reagan mode. We always competed for soft drinks.

While Kevin coaxed change out of his pocket, I thought about the Ultimate Final Championship again, trying to remember who won. I sat on the bench near the first tee.

I suddenly remembered Reagan sitting on a Beach Ball bench with a few holes to go last summer. Right after she had taken a late lead. She said she needed to rest, which was odd. She never stopped playing anything, especially when she had the momentum. She honored momentum like it was a special god.

I shivered. Maybe that was Reagan's heart starting to go bad.

I stared into the distance, past the farmhouse on the hill, and tried to remember what happened during the last few holes of the Ultimate Final Championship.

I couldn't.

"Sam?" asked Kevin. He held two Diet Cokes. "You okay?"

"Yeah, sure," I said.

He gave me the Maddie-and-Jonesy look that said such moments were okay.

"Come on," I said. "I have a match to win."

"Oh, we decided on match play?" said Kevin.

"What do you mean?"

"Match play is hole by hole, and medal play is total strokes."

"Right," I said. "What might feel less humiliating?"

"Match play," Kevin said.

"Okay," I said. "Let's do that so you don't have to hang your head when I destroy you."

"Fine with me, but I wouldn't count those chickens," said

Kevin. "But you do still have honors." He pointed at the first hole again. "Show me the way."

We stepped over to the first tee.

He paused at the rack of putters. "Maybe I should make a change."

"Can you change equipment in a real golf match?" I asked.

"No," said Kevin.

"Then come on," I said.

The first hole was the easiest one, with all but a grooved path to the cup, but thinking about Reagan must have gotten my brain in a tizzy because I pulled the ball left and missed. Kevin nailed his putt, clinking the middle of the cup. So much for my lead. I directed him to the next hole with my arm out, palm up.

A carload of twelve-year-old boys unloaded outside the fence.

"Fans?" Kevin asked.

"They should watch and learn," I said.

Kevin made the next putt and so did I. We stayed tied for the next bunch of holes, making several key putts despite having to concentrate through the whoops and hollers of the boys now on the course. Kevin barely missed a hole in one on the windmill hole, and I sank mine to take the lead again.

"You realize you play best on the hard holes," he said.

"The thrill of competition," I said.

"Unbelievable."

The match came down to the signature silo hole. If I made it, I won, no matter what he did.

"What are the chances that you beat me on this hole twice in a row?" he said.

"Trying to psych me out?" I asked.

He shook his head.

"Because that makes me concentrate better."

"Uh-oh," said Kevin.

With honors, I went first. I stood at the tee, leaning left and then right to decide if I should stick with the chicken coop or be daring and prove my worth with the horse trough.

"And it looks like our leader is having a little trouble deciding on her approach shot," Reagan whispered.

I smiled. I turned away from Kevin. "Stop it," I whispered back. "And what are you doing here, anyway?"

"Will she go with the proven chicken coop bank, or challenge herself to take the match by hammering the tricky horse trough?" said Reagan.

I took a few steps away from the tee.

"Getting nervous?" asked Kevin.

"Never," I said. "Figuring out the biggest bang for the win."

"Samantha Wilson, with her nerves of steel, is likely fashioning a shot for the ages," whispered Reagan.

I took a deep breath. And then the final holes of the Ultimate Final Championship flooded into my head. I had tied it on the thirty-fifth hole. And then I had made a hole in one, for the first time ever, on the double-windmill, swooping-seagull eighteenth. It happened so rarely that they added me to the list of names on the bulletin board. And then we had packed the car and driven home, and Reagan had slept the entire way.

I had sat there smugly with my certificate of Beach Ball Adventure Golf fame while Reagan's heart was conking out. God.

"But after conquering the double-windmill, swooping-seagull hole at the seaside links, does Wilson really have anything left to prove?" Reagan whispered.

I pretended to sneeze so I could turn away from Kevin again.

"I remembered," I told Reagan. "You didn't feel good on the way home from the beach."

"Hit the shot," Reagan said.

"But maybe . . ."

"Hit the dang shot," said Reagan.

I gritted my teeth. I went to the ball, looked left and looked right, and then I hit the horse trough in the dead center. Hard. The ball careened beyond the silo, entered the corral through the swinging gate, and had so much spin that it hit the back of the cup and circled it three times before it came to a stop. In the cup.

Kevin's mouth dropped open.

"Bravo," said Reagan. "Bravo."

Kevin threw his hands in the air. "How?"

"I'll see you later," said Reagan.

I smiled.

"I can't believe you did that on both sides," said Kevin. He raised his arms straight up and bowed.

The double-windmill, swooping-seagull hole was harder.

Much harder. And then it dawned on me that the Final Ulti-mate Championship last summer had been the final ultimate championship. I would never play mini golf with Reagan again.

"You won!" said Kevin. "Why aren't you celebrating?"

I tried to smile through the latest psychic pain. "I was thinking about Reagan."

"Oh," said Kevin. "That's right, you said you guys played at the beach."

"We played everything everywhere," I said.

"I'm sorry about Reagan," said Kevin.

"Me too," I said.

We walked silently to the putter rack and replaced our putters. The pack of boys exploded in wild shouts when some-one knocked the ball in the cup. Up until then it had looked more like they were playing marbles with golf balls.

Kevin pointed to the drink machine. "Another one?"

I shook my head.

"Want me to see if she has candy bars or chips in that shack?"

"No thanks."

We stood still and watched the boys jog from the sixth hole straight to the ninth hole.

"Customers must play the course in order," the girl announced over a loudspeaker attached to a nearby tree.

"But there's no one else out here," yelled a tow-haired kid in a Patriots sweatshirt.

"And if you don't follow the rules, there'll be no one at all," came her response, a little louder.

Kevin and I laughed.

"I am sorry about Reagan," he said. "It must be so hard."

I shrugged.

"She was really special."

"You talk like you knew her," I said.

He reddened. "It's what everyone says."

His eyes blinked.

"There's more to it than that," I said. He had always known a little too much about me, and now Reagan.

He sighed.

"And?" I said.

"And I went to preschool with Reagan," he said. "When we were four years old."

I couldn't believe it. He knew Reagan before I did.

"She was amazing," he said. "She ruled our class."

My face froze in disbelief.

The boys ran to the seventh hole.

"I decided she was my girlfriend," he said. "I gave her a Valentine's card that year, well, a special one since we had to give cards to all the kids in class, and I mailed her one every year after that until I was in middle school."

I remembered the cards. Reagan thumbtacked them on her bulletin board but wouldn't tell me anything more. She said that every girl should have a secret admirer and the operative word was "secret." I snuck in her room once and opened one card. It was signed *K*.

"You weren't in kindergarten with us, were you?" I asked.

It seemed like a kid dressed in black would have stood out.

"No," said Kevin. "We moved to Boston so Dad could go to grad school."

He smiled. "And every year, Mom would take me to the post office after school and I'd mail a Valentine's Day card to Reagan."

I put my putter back in the rack.

"When did you come back here?" I asked.

"Sixth grade," said Kevin.

He put his putter back.

"And it crossed my mind that it would be cool if we ended up in school together again, but we moved to a house near Carlow Community, where my dad got a teaching job."

The South End. Different schools.

Kevin shook his head. "And then, you know, preschool is ancient history when you're in sixth grade."

"You stopped sending the cards," I said. I remembered that I looked for one on Valentine's Day in sixth grade and there was no new secret admirer card. "You made her sad," I said.

Kevin looked at me in horror. "I—well, it seemed weird after we moved back here."

I glared at him.

"But I never forgot Reagan, and when I saw her name in the paper for basketball, I started to look for it."

I shook my head.

"I had this crazy idea that I'd go to a high school game to watch her play and she'd see me from the floor and remember me."

"I had this crazy idea that I'd go to high school and play with her," I said.

Kevin frowned. "I'm sorry," he said. "I don't mean to make you sad."

"I'm always sad," I said.

"I couldn't believe she died. I saw it in the paper, and I couldn't believe it."

I walked to my bike, and Kevin followed me.

"I should have told you," he said.

"So what, Reagan's the reason you were nice to me with the metal detector?"

"What?" he said.

"You heard me."

"I didn't know you'd lost the half hearts. I just knew you'd lost something." He paused. "And I sure didn't know it was a keepsake from Reagan."

"But you knew Reagan was my friend, right?"

He shrugged. "Some kids were talking about you when you didn't show up for the first day of school. They said you were taking Reagan's death hard."

"That's right," I said. "She was my best friend, not some fantasy from preschool."

Kevin started to say something, but he stopped. "I know."

"So you were interested in me because of Reagan?"

"No," Kevin said. He paused. "Well, maybe."

"So you wanted to get to know Reagan's friend after she died? Even though you haven't laid eyes on Reagan since she was four years old? Could you be any more creepy?"

"I am not creepy!" he yelled.

The boys stopped trash-talking and stared at us.

The loudspeaker made a scratchy sound and then the girl announced, "Customers are not allowed to loiter after they have finished play."

Kevin looked like he could strangle her.

I stared at Kevin's black ensemble. His black cap actually had a skull and bones on it. No. Not creepy at all.

I picked up my bike. "Give me a head start," I said. "And then don't follow me."

"Sam," he said.

"Ten minutes. Don't you dare touch your bike for ten minutes."

Fuming, I jumped on my bike and pedaled away as fast as I could.

———————————

I paged through my geometry book. But that made me think about Kevin even more than I was already thinking about Kevin, and I opened my Spanish book instead. Two quizzes marked C-minus fell out of it, along with three lists of vocabulary words from last week. I really needed to catch up on my schoolwork. I was so mad at Kevin that I couldn't sit still, but I fidgeted my way through several weeks' worth of Spanish vocabulary to think about something else. I waited for words like "jerk" or "loser" to show up, but the lists didn't include such useful terms.

Dad knocked on the door. "Sweetie?"

"Come in."

Dad opened the door. "That boy Kevin called the house line," he said.

I looked at my phone. Three calls and two texts from Kevin asking me to call him.

"I'm busy studying," I said.

"I'll take a message," Dad said.

"No need," I said. "I'll see him at school on Monday."

Dad gave me his concerned look, but he said, "Okay."

I gave up on homework and lay on my bed. I wanted Kevin to leave me alone.

I stared at the Dribble Queen team picture. You would think homework would be more productive without the constant interruptions from Reagan asking which assignment was due when, and did I think that was a seriously drop-dead date or was it one of those close-enough dates? We had never had a close-enough-due-date teacher, so the entire concept was this farfetched dream of Reagan's.

That was never going to come true.

"Crap!" I yelled.

"Language," said Reagan.

"That's not so bad."

"The people I'm with now have high standards," said Reagan.

"Well, I wish you'd told me about the people I'm with now," I said.

"What do you mean?" asked Reagan.

"I mean Kevin. Why didn't you tell me he was your pre-school heartthrob?"

"First of all, you've got that reversed. He had a crush on me."

"My apologies."

"Second of all, how the heck did I know Goth Boy Kevin was Kevin from preschool? He's ten years older and like three times bigger!"

"Still."

"Still what?" Reagan said. "Give me a break."

"Okay, okay."

"He was a weird little guy that the other kids didn't like. I was nice to him."

"He's still a weird guy," I said.

"I suppose," said Reagan. "But he helped you find the half hearts."

"He found the half hearts," I said.

"He's not a bad guy," said Reagan.

"The whole thing is creepy."

"I can't help it if he was intrigued with me. I can't help it if I was a preschool star," Reagan said.

"I wish someone was intrigued with me."

"Who says he isn't?"

I grabbed the pillow and held it tight. "I want my own intrigue. Not hooked-to-you intrigue. I want people to like me for me."

"Are those lyrics to a new song?" Reagan asked.

"Stop it."

"You're right. It's too sappy for that."

There was another knock at the door. "Sam?" said Dad.

"Yeah?"

"Are you okay? Bradley says you're talking to yourself and he can't go to sleep."

"Really?"

"Which doesn't explain why he's bouncing on his bed."

"Must be the radio, Dad," I said. "I'll turn it off."

"Thanks, sweetie," Dad said. "And Bradley's bed thanks you."

"Sure."

"Holy moly," I said after Dad walked down the hall.

"And when did Moly get special status?" asked Reagan.

"God."

"He would know about such things," said Reagan. "I could ask."

I burst out laughing.

"Laughing at the Lord isn't going to help," whispered Reagan. "Keep it down."

"I like Kevin," I whispered. "Well, I did like him. But I want people to live in the present with me and not in the past with you."

She says in a conversation with her dead friend.

"That didn't come out right," I said.

"Figured," said Reagan.

"I don't know what to do," I said.

"At least you can do something," said Reagan.

My self-pity slammed me.

I sighed. "I'm sorry, Reagan."

"I know," she said. "And it's okay."

"Really?"

"Not much I can do about it."

I nodded.

"Look, I need to go."

"You aren't mad at me, are you?"

"I just need to go."

And then she left, and then I felt that sunken feeling I always got when she left me. Like I had swum so far down in a lake that it was pitch-black.

And that was way too dark for homework.

I shut off the light and tried to go to sleep.

MONDAY, MONDAY

Monday morning, I loaded the books that hadn't seen much of me into my backpack. They seemed to be getting heavier. I would have to keep lifting weights to carry them.

I didn't move when Luke parked the truck. I wondered if being on school grounds was all that mattered for attendance. Maybe I could sit in the parking lot until Spanish and geometry were over. No vocabulary quiz and no Kevin.

Luke stood outside his opened door. "Coming?" he asked.

I shrugged.

He shook his head. "Well, lock it if you decide to further your education."

He slammed his door shut and jogged to catch up to friends who parked in the vicinity of the school building.

I considered the relative difficulty of sitting next to Kevin versus dealing with school security spotting me in Luke's truck.

It was a toss-up. I went with classes.

My burst of Spanish homework that weekend was useful, and I managed to write several answers during the vocabulary quiz, much to the surprise of Señora Schmidt, whose name I finally learned. And yes, she was hired to teach German and got stuck with Spanish I due to last-minute budget cuts. As the class neared bell time, I thought about Betsy Bowright from first grade, who was able to vomit at will. I could use a stint in the nurse's office during geometry.

The bell rang, and I stood quickly, hoping that a little dizziness would bring on nausea. Nothing. I headed for the hall, disappointed in my stomach. I thought about how angry Mom got when she had to come pick me and Reagan up during the Tour de Vanilla. She lectured us, as we held our upset stomachs in the back seat, on how we were inviting chronic diseases with our sugar intakes. Reagan had said, "Okay, you win. No more chocolate sprinkles on my hot-fudge sundaes."

I smiled.

"Thinking about that approach shot off the horse trough?" asked Kevin, who fell into step beside me.

The smile ended.

"It was amazing, Sam," he said. "Truly amazing."

I still didn't say anything.

"Look, I'm sorry," he said.

I picked up the pace.

"I helped you at the field because you seemed so upset about losing something," he said. "And I liked you and that's why I wanted to hang out with you."

"Right."

"And you are so much fun at golf and you are so athletic," he said.

"Just like Reagan," I said.

"We didn't play sports in preschool," said Kevin.

"Are you telling me she didn't shine in Simon Says?"

"Okay. The teacher let her run Simon Says."

I shook my head. I looked away.

We got stuck behind half the football team. Occasionally they sped up to sauntering.

"Reagan was cool," Kevin said. "I figured I'd like any friend of hers."

"I like to figure out my friends myself," I said.

Kevin shook his head. "Nothing I say will help, will it?"

I shrugged.

"It's this freaking school," he said. "It sucks, and nothing will change that." He shook his head. "Absolutely nothing."

"What?" I asked. I may have been the reason school didn't work for me, but I definitely wasn't the reason school didn't work for him. Maybe his antisocial attitude, but not me.

"I've had it with this freaking place," he said. His face turned popping red.

He tried elbowing his way past the offensive line, but he couldn't make headway. So he pushed an unsuspecting Jim Dawson, tight end, and squeezed between him and Rocky Dent, extra wide tackle, and stormed down the hall, pushing a few other students out of the way as well.

"What the hell!" yelled Rocky.

"Stupid move, man!" yelled Jim.

"Kevin," I yelled. "Wait up!"

But he had already ducked into geometry class. When the football clot dissolved, I rushed into the room. Where he sat, eyes straight ahead.

"Kevin," I said. "What was that all about?"

He didn't move.

Other students walked in and took their seats.

"Kevin!"

Brain D. put his books under his chair and looked at him. "Dude, I'd talk to her if I were you."

But Kevin just stared at the whiteboard. He was still staring at it when Mr. Pratt began to mumble.

I slumped in my seat.

At lunch, I focused on not provoking an instant message from Team NSA. I had managed not to say anything incendiary lately, and Mom hadn't come home early in ages. I had thought of stalking Rick Roberts to have something to add to the conversation, but I figured the depressed girl on a watch shouldn't add to her questionable behaviors.

"How's the Blizzard doing?" I asked.

"Well, we really don't have a point guard," said Maddie. "I mean, there's Lilly Myers, and Coach is trying her there, but well, you know . . ."

"She's really not a point guard," I said.

I played with my mashed potatoes.

"Hey, I'm not trying to dis you," said Maddie. "I understand why you're not playing."

"We do understand," Jonesy said.

"And we kept hearing about this new girl who was supposed to try out, but she never showed up," said Maddie.

Jonesy shrugged. "She moved here, and rumor was her parents wanted her to focus on school."

"Here? At Carlow High?" I asked.

Jonesy shrugged. "Don't know if she's here or at Bishop Hardy."

"Well, I am running," I said. "And lifting weights."

Jonesy and Maddie perked up.

"That's great," said Maddie. "You'll be ready for school tryouts."

I nodded. But it was the nod of knowing I had no such intention.

"You could probably come to some Blizzard practices, if you wanted," said Jonesy.

I didn't respond.

There was a tap on my shoulder. I turned to find Kevin, the last person I expected to see. He was breathless.

"Hey," he said. "Have you seen my notebook anywhere?"

"Geometry notes?" I asked.

"No," he said. "I don't even try to take notes in that class."

Maddie and Jonesy shook their heads. Everyone knew about Mr. Pratt.

"My sketchbook," he said. "You know, my drawings."

"No," I said. "I haven't seen it."

"Crap," he said. "I thought I might have left it in geometry." He blew out a long breath. "I've looked everywhere. The halls, the bathroom, my locker, everywhere I could think."

"Sorry," said Maddie.

"Is there a lost and found?" I asked.

"I doubt it," Kevin said. He hurried away.

"What's that about?" asked Jonesy.

"He's an artist," I said.

"That explains the clothes," said Maddie.

"And he draws all the time in that sketchbook," I said. "I've seen his work. He's really good."

"I hope he finds it," Jonesy said.

I did, too. Even though I was not happy with Kevin, I didn't want him to lose his art. Especially after he found the half hearts. I owed him forever for that.

I reached up and felt them.

"Hey," said Maddie. "Is this the week we get preview grades?"

"What?" I asked. "I thought report cards came out the middle of November."

"They do," said Maddie. "But they give previews to freshmen when grades close, which I think is Friday."

"That's right," said Jonesy. "It was in the information packet."

I panicked. I had done little or no work so far. I had wondered why teachers weren't hammering me for it, but maybe in high school they wait until the first report card because a line of Fs sends the message just fine.

I was in so much trouble.

"Hey, what's he doing?" I heard someone yell.

Kids moved to the windows on the side of the cafeteria.

Jonesy stood. "Hey, Sam, it's Kevin. In the fountain."

I jumped up.

It was indeed Kevin standing in the fountain near the school entrance, picking up pages that must have been torn from his sketchbook. He'd grab one, shake water off it, and place it on the stone wall surrounding the fountain. The football players in the hallway must have gotten their revenge quickly.

"I can't believe they did that," I said.

Students rushed to the windows. Luke and Brain D. ran outside.

The lunch bell rang.

"Okay, okay, it's time for class," Principal Carson yelled. He stood at the edge of the cafeteria with folded arms.

More students walked to the windows.

Luke and Brain D. jumped into the fountain and helped Kevin pick up his sketches before they were completely ruined. I swear Kevin looked straight at me and then looked away.

And I didn't blame him. He was trying to apologize that morning, and I was a jerk. He wouldn't have made those stupid football players mad if I had only been polite. It wasn't his fault that Reagan captivated him. And it wasn't her fault that she died and created this whole miserable mess with me and him.

It was my fault.

"I WILL give detentions!" Mr. Carson yelled.

Kids collected their books.

"I want to see some URGENCY!" Mr. Carson yelled again.

Students walked past me, but I just stood there.

I couldn't do anything right. I was about to get the worst grades in the history of the Wilson family. I was lying to Maddie and Jonesy about going out for school basketball—my team-mates who stuck with me no matter how I treated them. And now this guy who was only trying to be nice to me was holding his ruined art.

Even Dead Reagan was mad at me.

I was worthless.

STARRY AFTERNOON

I waited for Maddie and Jonesy at the lunch line on Wednesday. I had collected previews of all my grades except geometry.

I had straight Cs. That's like straight As without the As.

Silverware clanged on the floor when a kitchen aide lost his grip on a tray.

I didn't know why my grades weren't all Fs. The most work I'd done was the mini binge on Spanish vocabulary. I had two weeks to prepare Mom and Dad for the report card that would show up in our mailbox. I doubted they would be as nice as the teachers giving phantom Cs to the kid with the dead friend. It seemed that their generous interpretation of classroom participation included sitting up straight.

At the table, Jonesy dissected her vegetarian quesadilla. Four slices of pepper, two chunks of tomato, two pieces of possibly eggplant, and ten shreds of unmelted cheese. So maybe because that made my own quesadilla less appealing, or maybe because I wanted to head off a discussion about grades, or maybe because I simply wasn't good with guilt, I blurted, "You know, I don't think I'm going to play basketball at all this year."

Maddie looked up from her quesadilla. "You mean, not even high school?"

I nodded.

"Just too hard without, you know . . . ?" asked Jonesy.

"Right," I said.

"We understand," said Maddie.

"We do," said Jonesy. She put down her dissecting fork and picked up her apple.

I didn't understand. I expected a reaction. That I'd led them on, that it was time to get my act together, that Lilly Myers didn't even go to Carlow High and that point guards didn't grow on trees. That I had an obligation. That enough was enough.

"But—" I said.

"Hey, we get it," said Maddie.

"And Starr will do fine at point," said Jonesy.

Bingo.

"Starr?" I asked.

Maddie nodded. "Sophomore transfer," she said. "That kid who couldn't go out for the Blizzard? Her parents are letting her play school ball. And lucky us, she goes here."

"Where's she from?" I asked.

"California," said Jonesy.

"And you're telling me today?" I asked.

"I just found out this morning," said Jonesy. "In gym class."

"Well, she's been in your gym class all along," Maddie said.

"Right. But we came indoors today, you know, Coach Gray keeps everyone playing soccer. But since it's raining, we played basketball." Jonesy bit into her apple. And then she chewed and swallowed. "Coach Gray found out she's assistant basketball coach, so she needs the practice."

"She's a good soccer coach," said Maddie.

"Well, I'm not sure she held a basketball before today," said Jonesy.

"So Starr's good?" I asked.

"Amazing," said Jonesy. "I mean, she looked like some goof when we played soccer. But, man, put a basketball in her hands and she turns into a machine."

"A scoring machine," said Maddie. "We looked her up in French class. She was lead scorer on her AAU team in California for three straight years."

I had been lead scorer for the Blizzard for three straight years. Only because Reagan mostly played point and set me up. Otherwise, she would have been high scorer. One of us would always be the high scorer. Not some beach baby named Starr.

Jonesy noticed my scowl. "Well, I'm sure she didn't score as many points as you did."

That was better.

"We want you to play, we really do!" said Maddie. "That would be killer, you and Starr! You know . . ."

"Maddie," said Jonesy.

I got it. It would be like me and Reagan, without the Reagan.

"She didn't miss this morning," said Jonesy. "We nicknamed her Shooting Starr, get it?"

"What's her last name?" I asked.

"Regal," said Jonesy.

"Starr Regal? That sounds like a porn name," I said.

"She doesn't play like a porn star," said Jonesy.

"Like you would know how a porn star plays basketball," said Maddie.

Jonesy laughed. "Didn't your brother get caught with the basketball edition of a girlie magazine?"

"Stuck inside a *Highlights* magazine," said Maddie.

They both laughed hysterically.

I didn't think it was funny.

And as much as I couldn't deal with playing basketball without Reagan, I couldn't deal with some out-of-town chick named Starr taking our place. I reached up and grabbed the half hearts. This time, they did not make me feel better. I pushed my chair back.

"Aren't you going to eat?" asked Maddie.

"Not hungry," I said.

"I shouldn't have said anything," said Jonesy. "Starr probably had beginner's luck today."

"It's okay," I said.

But it wasn't.

I picked up my tray and started to walk away. But then I looked back.

"When are tryouts again?"

"Tuesday," said Jonesy.

I pounded the basketball on the driveway.

"Come on, Bradley," I yelled. "Push me."

"That would be a foul," he said.

"In baby basketball, maybe," I said. "Not the real stuff."

"I don't play baby basketball," said Bradley.

"Just play something," I said.

He shrugged and guarded me again. He leaned into my side.

"Good," I said.

I rolled around him, pounded my way to the basket, and scored with a layup. Six inches shorter than me, Bradley wasn't much competition, but some pressure was better than none. We'd been playing in the driveway since I got home from school. I was sweating, so I pulled off my fleece pullover.

I couldn't believe it, but I was thinking of trying out. The idea of someone named Starr taking over the space that was rightfully mine and Reagan's was not sitting well.

It was either play or break her leg.

Luke drove partly into the driveway.

I pointed to the street, his designated parking spot when the driveway was in play.

"What's going on?" he asked.

I glared at him.

He put the truck in reverse and shot back out.

"Come on," said Bradley when Luke walked up. "Take my place."

Luke put his backpack on the steps, and Bradley sat beside it. Luke tossed off his field jacket and his sweater. I held the ball against my hip, waiting. He stretched his arms over his head, flexed from side to side, and then pulled his keys from his pocket and tossed them to Bradley.

"Not that I won't be driving on you," he said.

"Who said you'd get the ball?" I said.

"Whoa," said Bradley. "This is going to be good."

As soon as Luke got set to defend me, I put the ball in play and went hard for the basket. I put in a right-handed layup without so much as a glance at the backboard.

"I wasn't ready," said Luke.

"Neither was I."

We played one-on-one for half an hour. Luke had to back off a bit to make it fair, since he was a lot stronger and taller, but there were stretches where we both went all out. We played without anything but sound-bite trash talk. Bradley provided a play-by-play commentary for a few minutes, but he got bored and went inside the house. He reappeared eventually and placed bottles of Gatorade on the steps, a household tradition when we engaged in personal combat.

Luke and I took a break and grabbed the bottles.

"Starr Regal?" Luke asked, still breathing hard.

"Maybe," I said. I chugged the ice-blue drink. "She really good?"

Luke nodded. "Saw her play at the Community Center. But she's not as good as you and Reagan."

"Really?" I said. I liked that Luke never avoided saying Reagan's name.

"She'll make the team," Luke said. "But you should be starting point guard." He finished off his drink and pounded it on the porch. "If you want it."

I wanted it. All of a sudden, I really wanted it.

"Come on," I said.

We headed back to the driveway and worked on jump shots until it got too dark. And then Luke turned on the lights and we practiced foul shots until Bradley called us in for dinner.

That night, I figured I better make some last-ditch effort in geometry. I had caught up to early October in assignments when Reagan showed up.

"You need to work on your crossover dribble left," she said.

"You always say that."

"It always needs to be said."

"I might try out," I said. "I'm not that rusty."

"You have to play," said Reagan.

I waited for the rest. That I had to play because she couldn't.

But Reagan didn't say anything else.

"I'm a little worried about this Starr chick," I said.

"Twinkle, twinkle, little star?"

I laughed. "Actually, I think she goes by Twinkie."

"Except when you get to know her. Then it's Twink. You know, Twink, Twink, little star. How I wonder what you are."

I burst out laughing.

"And her close friends call her Twinks."

"Of course."

"Hey," Mom said from the hall. "Is Bradley in there with you?"

Yikes. "No, Mom, I'm on the phone."

"Nice touch," whispered Reagan.

"Shh!"

"Oh, well, that's nice," said Mom. "But it's past ten, so it's time to shut things down."

"Okay," I said. "Night."

"Geez," I said to Reagan. "I need to be more careful."

"They think you're crazy, anyway," said Reagan.

"You're crazy."

"No. I'm dead. You don't get to be both crazy and dead."

I couldn't wrap my head around that. I put my geometry book on my desk and got into bed. My body was good and tired for the first time in months. Running is great, but it's not like playing a real sport. I was going to sleep well.

"Hey, I'll make the team, right?" I asked Reagan.

"Are we playing silly questions?"

"I'm rusty," I said.

"You looked good against Luke. Just work on moving left, like always. And the crossover dribble left, like always."

"Will you come watch tryouts?" I asked.

"Sure," said Reagan. "Night for now."

I lay there getting excited about the tryout. And nervous, although I didn't know why. Heck, the wrap-up newspaper story on the team's so-so season last winter ended by saying that their fortunes would be reversed once Reagan Murphy and Samantha Wilson showed up. I tried not to mind that it was always Reagan first, since she won with superior alphabetical order on both first and last names.

M and W. Upside down and right side up.

Then I felt the air get sucked out of me. It was supposed to be Reagan and me. Every day last summer when we rode our bikes past the high school gym, Reagan would point and say, "You. Will. Be. Our. Stage." And we would high-five, almost falling off the bikes a couple times. I told Reagan that if she broke her leg, she wouldn't be on that stage. Who knew it was her heart that was broken.

I walked to the window and rolled up the shade. The night was cold and clear, and the stars and the full moon shined bright. I fingered my half hearts and wondered where Reagan went when she left me.

Up above the world so high,

Like a diamond in the sky.

I got back in bed and pulled up the covers. I was so tired that I could feel myself fade away when I hit the pillow. And I slept the sleep of the dead by the living.

SLIDE, ANGEL, SLIDE

I sat in geometry class with a month's worth of homework shoved in my backpack. I had thought about handing it to Mr. Pratt at the beginning of class, but I didn't want to attract attention. I didn't need to announce to my classmates that I hadn't done a lick of work, especially if Pratt was giving me the depressed C like the other teachers.

I stole a glance at Kevin, who was even more quiet than usual. A new sketchbook lay on his desk, but it was shut. He stared at the whiteboard.

Mr. Pratt picked up a file folder. "Class," he said, "I have some administrative details before I can begin instruction today. The school requires me to provide the freshmen with preview grades this week."

I figured it was way too late to pray.

"I have a yellow sticky for each freshman," he said. He looked at senior Brain D. and shook his head.

Mr. Pratt proceeded alphabetically, and I could barely

breathe when he hit the middle of the alphabet and made the turn to the later letters, like "W" for "Wilson." Please give me that depressed C, I thought. I swore I would never put myself in the position of hoping for a C again. Depressed or otherwise.

Kevin made a tiny airplane out of his preview sticky and flew it into the wastebasket near the front desk. I could only imagine what Pratt wrote on that one.

I shifted in my seat. I should have handed him the homework. I should have come to school early and gotten on my knees and begged him to look at my work. Surely proving that I now knew the material, or at least the September material, would count for something.

Mr. Pratt slapped a yellow sticky on my desk. I had no idea they could make so much noise.

I exhaled loudly. Then I peeled it open.

D-minus.

In Sharpie-screaming red. Mr. Pratt must have pressed down hard to make the letter so bold.

This was bad.

I was in so much trouble. I'm not sure my mother knew about grades that low. She and Dad made Luke stop playing travel basketball because he came home with two Cs his freshman year.

At least they couldn't make me quit the Blizzard.

Apparently no one talked to Mr. Pratt about taking it easy on the student with a dead friend. He wouldn't exactly be a magnet in the faculty lounge. Or maybe he thought a "D" for "depressed" was amusing.

Geometry wasn't even that hard. I had waltzed through those assignments last night.

Oh God.

Mr. Pratt stood in front of the class.

"I am required to inform you that high school requires a certain adjustment, and that the first-quarter grades are often a surprise to students used to a certain level of performance," he said.

"You aren't kidding," said someone behind me.

"But three quarters remain in the school year, and that's plenty of time to bring your grades up to more acceptable levels," he said. He looked at Kevin. "Although that may require some changes."

If looks could kill—Kevin's bored a hole through Mr. Pratt's skull.

I tried to think. Grades didn't actually close until the end of the day. Maybe I could spend study hall and lunch adding to the completed assignments from last night and get the D-minus up to a D. Or even a C-minus. That would make Mom and Dad so proud.

"One more thing," said Mr. Pratt. "To avoid any misunderstanding. Nothing can be done about your quarter grades. That's why I wait to the very last day of the preview period." He smirked. "It makes it easier for both of us."

So much for the last-day rush.

I sat back as Mr. Pratt switched to mumble mode to begin the day's lesson.

Kevin looked like he was plotting Pratt's demise in the most painful way possible, and Brain D. played some kind of flicker spitball game on his desk. He turned to show off his work, with blue-and-black-inked spitballs lined up on what appeared to be a basketball court in his notebook, complete with out-of-bounds and free-throw lines.

Oh God, I thought. What if my grades made me ineligible for playing basketball? Never mind my parents, schools had rules about this stuff.

I panicked. My straight As in middle school hadn't prepared me for eligibility issues. It seemed like one kid or another was dropped from Charger teams for academic reasons, but I thought that was for flunking. But then again, middle school and high school were different. I didn't know if that was good or bad for me.

Brain D. got excited. He turned to show me that he had flicked all the blue balls into the tiny circle that must have been the goal.

"Awesome," I whispered.

Then it dawned on me. Brain D. would know the eligibility rules.

"Brian," I whispered. "What are the rules for grades to play a sport?"

He put his hand up and then wrote a note. When Pratt turned his back to write more gibberish on the whiteboard, he passed it to me.

Brain D. knew his stuff.

Nothing less than a D, and only one grade less than a C. The D must become a C or higher in order for the athlete to continue playing sports in the subsequent quarter. Minuses and pluses do not make any difference.

Minuses didn't matter. I could play basketball.

I gave a fist pump under my desk.

And then my grades floated into my head. Four Cs and a D-minus.

Well, I could play until my parents found out.

When class ended, I threw my folder of old homework into the trash basket.

TRYING

On Tuesday, I kept my eyes on Mr. Pratt, with my hand resting on the page that seemed like the day's topic. And I visualized my basketball tryout, on tap for that afternoon. But Reagan kept crashing my daydreams. Either we were exchanging passes, or I was taking the wing as she drove the middle on a fast break, or she yelled, "In. The. Hoop!" when I launched a promising shot.

My brain just didn't process basketball without her. There was the ball and the basket and Reagan.

"Mr. Holt?" said Mr. Pratt. "Is there a reason you are staring at Ms. Wilson instead of me?"

God. My face turned into a Vivid Violet crayon. I didn't have to look at Kevin to know we had a matching set.

"She is a lot prettier," said Brain D.

The class collectively giggled.

Mr. Pratt scowled. "I asked Mr. Holt, not you, Mr. Dowling."

"Oh," Brain D. said.

Scattered giggles.

Mr. Pratt frowned. "Mr. Holt?"

Kevin said nothing, as always.

"So I see your restraint from classroom communication extends past the mathematical to the personal," said Mr. Pratt.

It struck me that real words came out of Mr. Pratt's mouth only for the personal and not the mathematical.

Mr. Pratt took a few steps toward Kevin. "Okay, then, detention with me after school, Mr. Holt. Again."

Kevin didn't even acknowledge Pratt.

Brain D. turned slightly when Mr. Pratt picked up his marker. "Jerk," he whispered to the aisle.

Kevin shrugged.

I wrapped the half hearts around my deodorant stick and then zipped my duffel bag and shoved it into the gym locker.

"See you soon," I said.

"What?" asked Maddie, turning the corner from the other aisle of lockers.

"Nothing," I said.

"You ready?"

"Let's go," I said.

We walked into the gym, its floor still smooth and shiny from summer polishing and its red and blue lines sharp and bright. Clear weather had kept my gym class outside all fall, and I'd only stepped on the floor to get to the bleachers for a couple stupid assemblies. A shiver ran down my back and into my legs. This was to be our stage. Me and Reagan.

I bit my lip so I wouldn't cry.

Just keep breathing, I told myself.

Girls shot at the baskets, all six of which had been lowered. At the far end, a girl with bleach-blond hair practiced free throws. She wore a faded tank top, and her shoulders were still tanned. Another girl rebounded for her. One, two, three shots fell easily through the net.

I looked at Maddie.

She nodded. "That's Starr."

I did not like the girl I saw. I did not like her much at all.

Maddie ran to Jonesy's basket, but I just stood there. I watched Starr go through her moves: quick jump shot, reverse layup, between-the-legs dribble, and a fadeaway jumper. Every few shots, she took dance steps, as if listening to invisible headphones.

She never switched up and rebounded for her partner. Maybe Starr was too good for that.

I kept expecting to hear Reagan pipe up. She had promised. Instead, the whistle blew. Tryouts were on.

Coach Collins directed us to the bleachers. Two assistants stood next to him, clipboards in their hands. One was Coach Gray, in her soccer gear. The other was Mr. Falls, the handsome young math teacher who was rumored to enunciate all his words. He was the JV coach, which explained the presence of several freshman girls I hadn't seen on a basketball court since fifth grade.

"Tryouts today and tomorrow," Coach Collins said. "This way everyone gets a good look."

His assistants nodded.

"And we can probably get most of you on the JV team if you don't make varsity."

Some girls clapped. They probably expected participation trophies, too.

"So go hard," he said. "I want everyone competing for a slot on varsity." He smiled. "And that includes last year's team members! Nothing is guaranteed."

Coach Collins was good. Reagan and I had watched most of the home games last year. He pushed his players hard, but he wasn't a jerk. He never criticized them publicly, and he was quick to complain to a referee if the other team was getting away with dirty play. He'd mapped out a few last-minute plays that had been pure genius.

He looked my way and gave me the "sorry" stare.

I concentrated on my basketball shoes. I was having enough trouble keeping them on the court. I wondered if Coach Collins was feeling more sorry for me or for himself, losing a great guard like Reagan. Or maybe he'd already heard about Starr. Maybe he'd just crossed out Reagan on his tentative roster and substituted Regal—just another coach making a lineup change.

I teared up thinking about a line through Reagan's name.

I bit my lip again. There's no crying in basketball, I told myself.

I concentrated on breathing so hard that I was practically hyperventilating when Coach Collins blew the whistle again. He split us into two groups, with Starr in one and me in the other, and sent us to opposite ends of the gym.

I followed Coach Gray, hoping the pre-loaded oxygen wouldn't make me faint. We started with basic layup drills, switching from right-handed to left-handed after a few times through the lines. Then we moved to three-man weaves, speed dribbling, stop-and-start dribbling, and crossover dribbling. I wondered what tryout Reagan was attending since she was twenty minutes late for mine.

I kept listening for her voice, to the extent that I twice lost concentration on my crossover dribbling and fumbled the ball. That rated a notation on Coach Gray's clipboard. And the idea of some soccer player making remarks about my basketball skills was infuriating. Still fuming a few minutes later, I didn't hear the command to stop dribbling during a start-and-stop drill. I kept bouncing the ball when everyone else stopped. I felt like I was six years old and at my very first basketball practice.

Older players checked out Starr's performance when we took a break.

I was breathing hard. Too hard after a few lousy drills. So much for my recent running. I wiped sweat off my brow with my T-shirt.

Coach Gray made us line up across from each other, and we proceeded to passing drills. Chest passes, bounce passes, overhead passes, and baseball passes. I caught every ball and didn't throw anything over my partner's head. I was so proud.

Seriously, Reagan, I thought. Where are you? I can't do this without you and practice is half done.

Coach Gray split us into teams of two and reviewed the pick-and-roll play. We were to run through the play against our defenders five times and then switch offense and defense.

I took the ball, my teammate set a wide screen, and I drove around it and made a layup. The next time, she rolled off, and I found her for an easy jumper.

"That's how to execute!" said Coach Gray.

It's basic play, I thought. Give me a break.

We did exactly the same thing three more times, with Coach Gray getting more and more excited.

My drill teammate, a senior named Sandy, rolled her eyes at me when we switched to defense. "If she gets any more excited, we're going to have to call an ambulance."

"Just don't head the ball," I said. "She'll get so excited she'll go into convulsions."

Sandy burst out laughing, and so did Maya, a forward from last year's team.

Coach Gray gave me a strange look, like, "What, we've got a stand-up comic?"

I checked out the other group while the offense was getting set. Maddie saw me and waved. She and Jonesy had the privilege of trying out with the great Starr Regal. I'm surprised they didn't sell tickets. I watched Starr take the ball up top, ignore the screen, and drive for the hoop, slashing through last-minute defenders. She scored.

Showboat, I thought.

Coach Collins blew his whistle. "Nice creativity and I definitely want to see that in games," he said. "But let's stick to the drill."

I would have sat her down for that. But, hey, if he wants creativity—I can show him creativity.

"Samantha?"

Coach Gray stared at me.

"Let's focus on this drill, okay?"

"Yes, Coach."

I focused. I focused as much as a person can focus who's trying not to cry because her dead best friend didn't show up like she promised. At least I didn't have to worry that something had happened to her.

It already did.

By the time we scrimmaged, still kept in our groups, I was huffing and puffing like some middle-aged couch potato out for a hike with the grandkids. I was creatively trying not to fall down. I grabbed Sandy's jersey once to keep me up.

She looked at me, surprised.

"Hey, just wondered why you didn't play last year," I said quickly. "You're really good."

Sandy shook her head. "Busted my ACL right before the season," she said.

"Sucks," I replied.

She nodded.

Better a busted ACL than a busted heart, I thought. But I kept my mouth shut.

And wondered why Reagan hadn't shown up.

I played point for my side in the scrimmage, and I did manage to score one basket. But another shot from the top of the key fell flat, barely nudging the front of the rim.

"Work within your range," said Coach Gray.

I couldn't believe she said that.

The next time down the court, just to prove myself, I launched one from even farther out. The ball didn't come close to the hoop.

"That's outside your range," said Coach Gray, who then wrote something on her clipboard.

I couldn't play worse if I tried.

The other team held the ball until Coach Gray finished writing. I took a look at the other scrimmage. The great Starr Regal took on Jonesy on a fast break and juked her so bad that Jonesy ended up on her butt while Starr made an easy layup.

I hated Starr. But she was good.

"Samantha?" Coach Gray called. "This scrimmage."

I nodded and took the ball at the top again. I couldn't wait for practice to end.

ALONE AGAIN

When the final whistle blew, I rushed to the locker room. I didn't bother changing. I stuffed my clothes into my bag, grabbed my jacket, and marched to the back entrance. I was furious. I looked for Luke's truck, but it was gone. I thought about calling Mom or Dad, but I hadn't told them about trying out. The last thing I needed was their excitement at my triumphant return to the basketball court.

Triumphant like an elephant.

Geez, Reagan, I thought. How could you do that? All this talk about how you'll be there for me, and you don't show up.

It was freezing, so I stopped and put on my jacket. I didn't have gloves, so I jammed my hands into the pockets. I picked up the pace and nearly wiped out when I caught some ice on the sidewalk.

"Dang it," I said out loud.

"I'm sorry," said Reagan.

"What?"

"I'm sorry."

"I'm not talking to you," I said. I walked faster.

"Come on," she said.

"I was counting on you."

"I said I'm sorry."

"Well, I only tried out because you said you'd come."

I walked even faster. I was so mad. Although I didn't understand why it was so important to me that Reagan show up. I stopped letting my parents watch tryouts when I was ten years old. I needed to concentrate and not worry about anyone watching me. If I played my best, the coaches would know what to do.

Then there was today's performance. I'd played better for the Dribble Queen competition. And I sure didn't lose any balls on that crossover dribble.

"Slow down," said Reagan.

I walked faster.

And then I realized that I had never tried out without Reagan beside me. And I never worried about what she thought because I knew what she thought.

"Hey! Slow down. I'm dead—not bionic," said Reagan.

I still wasn't talking to her. But I slowed down.

Whenever I felt doubt, or messed up, or didn't feel my best, I could always take a look at Reagan and she would smile or make me laugh and I would feel stronger. I didn't need to build myself up because she did it for me.

I stood at the corner stop sign. No need to throw myself under a bus. Five o'clock traffic was under way, and a line of cars waited at the stop sign. Flurries made it seem even colder.

"Look," said Reagan. "First snow!"

"Just a few flurries," I said.

"The baddest nor'easter starts with a single snowflake."

"When did you start with the weather philosophy?" I asked.

"You get a good view from up there," Reagan said.

I nodded.

"I'd love a good foot of snow," said Reagan.

"We wouldn't have to study for Pratt's quiz tomorrow," I said.

"You wouldn't have to study for Pratt's quiz."

"Very funny."

"Remember how we used to make snow angels?"

"Sure," I said.

"Although I didn't realize I was practicing for my future."

I didn't say anything.

"Speaking of practice, I am sorry."

I shrugged.

"Look, I thought I was ready to be in a gym again, but I wasn't. I got all the way to the door, but it was too hard to hear balls bouncing and hitting the backboard. Then the whistle blew and I just couldn't go any farther."

She hesitated. "It's too soon."

This fierce chill ran down my head to my gut, freezing everything on the way. We hadn't talked about what happened the afternoon she died.

I closed my eyes. What a selfish person I was to expect Reagan to relive that to support me.

Traffic cleared, and we walked across the street.

"And at the same time, I miss playing ball so much," said Reagan. "Standing outside that door, it was like I remembered every minute of practice or games I'd ever played. And I missed the basketball I hadn't played yet. It was all so intense I couldn't take it. I had to go."

My eyes flooded. "I'm sorry."

"No, I'm sorry," Reagan said. "I didn't mean to leave you alone."

"I know," I said.

The flurries organized themselves, and we walked silently through a soft but steady snowfall. By the time we reached my front steps, the ground was white.

I wondered if snow covered her grave.

I stood there, freezing, with Dead Reagan. The falling snowflakes grew larger and larger.

"Smells like pot roast in there," she said.

"You can smell?"

"Yes. I can't fly, but I can smell."

"You can't eat, though, right?"

You could say I was met with dead silence.

"I'll give Mom your regrets," I said.

"I don't think I can make it tomorrow," Reagan said. "To practice."

"That's okay," I said.

"You better make the team."

"I will."

I could do this on my own. I had to do this on my own.

MAKING IT

I set my alarm for six the next morning. When it jarred me out of a deep sleep, I pulled on training pants, Reagan's hoodie, and a puff vest. I grabbed Dad's jogger headlight from his special drawer in the downstairs hallway. I was Samantha Wilson, lead scorer for the Blizzard, perennial winner of suicide drills, and the girl who wants the ball so bad when the game's on the line that she'll tear it out of a teammate's hands.

I needed to get my mojo back. I needed to chase it down no matter if it meant shin splints and side stitches from running too fast too early in the morning.

I opened the front door to find an inch of snow. I took a long breath of the arctic air. And I ran like crazy all the way to the entrance to Elliot Park, not stopping for stop signs or curbs or cats. Plan A was to turn around and run home, since even I wasn't stupid enough to run in the park before light, but the sun came up and the raspberry sky made everything all right.

I took two fast laps around the duck pond, and I did intervals all the way home.

Mom was stepping down the stairs when I opened the front door.

"What are you doing?" she asked. She wore her terrycloth bathrobe. Loops of hair fell out of the hair band she wore to bed.

"Getting an instant breakfast," I said. "Before I practice free throws."

"O-kay," Mom said. "I thought we were out."

"Secret stash."

"What?"

"There's no reason for not making a free throw," I said. "No reason at all."

She gave me the look that said my daughter has evolved from melancholy to mania. She made herself tea while I blended up a frothy instant breakfast.

I chugged it. Then I found a basketball in the garage and shot free throws until I made ten in a row. Then I started over and made another ten in a row, this time faster. And then I made ten layups in record time. And then I shot ten more free throws. And then I raced inside and up the stairs to get ready for school.

I was a different person at tryouts that afternoon. I was Sam-I-am Wilson. The coaches switched groups, and now I was under the watchful eye of Coach Collins. We practiced jumping for rebounds and defensive positioning. And then we practiced stop-and-starts and speed dribbling. We worked on boxing out until our butts were bruised. I didn't know how Twinks was doing with Coach Soccer Ball because I was totally focused on my play.

Coach Collins blew a long whistle.

I stood beside Maddie and Sandy, my shirt soaked and sweat dripping off my face.

"Okay," he said. "This is what you've all been waiting for! Final scrimmage!"

We cheered.

"That's right," he said. "It's showtime." He picked up the pile of green pinnies from the sideline. He motioned Mr. Falls to our group. "You're in charge of the green team," he said. "And, Coach Gray, you are the yellow coach." He picked up the yellow pinnies and gave them to her.

"Wilson, up top," Mr. Falls said to me.

I nodded.

"Big surprise," said Maddie.

He put Maddie at second guard and Sandy at center.

"Let's do it!" he said.

"Ah, assuming man-to-man?" said Sandy.

"Right," he said. "Yes."

Sandy rolled her eyes.

I didn't need further instruction. Reagan and I had attended enough games last year for me to know what Coach Collins liked. Guards up top pass and screen, and the forwards cut back and forth under the basket, looking for passes from the guards. Coach Collins decided to assess our fitness, so we played full court. Our green team took the ball out, and the yellow team matched up to pressure us. Starr took me on, and I immediately threw in the ball to Sandy and broke away from Starr for the return pass. Sandy nailed me, and I dribbled all the way down the floor to score.

"Nice!" yelled Sandy.

"Mark somebody," yelled Coach Gray.

Maddie laughed as we settled back to a half-court defense. "Her team's going to love the soccer talk!"

It didn't take much time for our green team to run up a 10–0 lead over the yellow team.

Then Starr convinced her side to stop listening to Coach Gray. They played a simple man-to-man defense beginning at half court and used the get-the-ball-to-Starr play on offense.

It worked. The girl could play basketball. She got me leaning the wrong way for her first basket. And then she pulled up way beyond the three-point line to score with a real bomb. Later, she nailed Prisha underneath to make an unexceptional backdoor cut look great. And she would have given them the lead if she had passed to one of two open players on another drive. Instead, she took the ball up the middle with three defensive players hanging on her and couldn't even get off a shot.

"Okay, let's stop there," said Coach Collins.

We took a water break, and then the subs entered the game. They played more selfishly than Starr, trying to be noticed.

After five minutes, the starters returned. Starr was lanky, but running into her screen told me she was packed with muscle. And she had quick hands, too, almost popping the ball away from me a couple times. She was definitely most comfortable with a playground style—showing off, making the big play, but often not knowing where her teammates were positioned.

Sandy shook her head when Starr lost her footing on yet another drive through the middle and she and two defenders ended up on the ground.

"She's really talented, but she's got some gaps," she said.

"She could play several positions," I said.

"Well, we need a point," she said. "And that's going to be you."

I didn't say anything. That was supposed to be Reagan.

I finished my Spanish vocabulary list and got into bed with my laptop. We were supposed to write an essay about *A Separate Peace*, but I couldn't get started. I had finally read the book last weekend so class made sense, but I couldn't think of a good topic. I should have been caught up in the facts that Gene loses his friend Finny, in more ways than one, and that Finny's heart stopped just like my best friend's heart stopped. Finny was a great athlete, and so was Reagan. Finny was full of life, and so was Reagan. Finny made up stupid games, and so did Reagan.

But I got stuck on the fact that Finny lived until he was a senior. Reagan didn't even get to be a freshman. Although Finny's broken leg did screw things up. But I'd sure as heck rather be pushing Reagan around in a wheelchair than doing this without her.

My screen saver turned itself on—now the Dribble Queen team picture that I had scanned. I studied my eight-year-old teammates surrounding Dribble Queen Reagan. I don't know that she would have been satisfied with a wheelchair.

Outside, a group of kids made their way down the street. It was well past Halloween, but I swear this one bunch was trolling for discarded candy. I heard them every night.

"And how did it go?" asked Reagan.

"What?"

"Tryouts, you fool."

"Thought you'd never ask."

"I can't believe you made that picture your screen saver." I shrugged.

"I'm only hoping your crossover went better today."

"Oh, it did," I said.

"Great."

"I missed you," I said.

"I know."

The screen saver gave up.

"So, how good is Twinks?" asked Reagan.

"She's good," I said. "She has some great moves and a really smooth shot. She can hit the long ones."

"But . . ."

"She can be undisciplined."

"It'll be interesting to see what Coach Collins does."

"You know it."

I hit the Return key to wake up the computer. I stretched my fingers.

"I get the hint," said Reagan.

"You can stay," I said. "But I need to write this essay."

"Don't forget geometry."

"Thanks for the reminder."

"Good night."

"Good night."

For the first time, I didn't feel that punch in the gut when Reagan left. I didn't know whether that was good or bad. I opened up a new file and typed "Finny."

The next morning, I walked to school early. I knew I must have made the team, but I needed to see it in person. The team roster was posted on Coach Collins's door and I was on it, along with Maddie, Jonesy, and Starr. Otherwise, the team included juniors and seniors. I leaned against the wall. I was pleased to have my name on the list, but it was a shock to see my first roster without Reagan Murphy.

I sank to a squat to absorb that.

I didn't know bittersweet could feel so bad.

FOOTBALL FOUNTAIN

Luke slammed his door shut.

"Don't forget the pep rally today," he said.

"How could I?" I asked. "It's required."

"Just pay attention," he said. He winked, and then he rushed ahead.

That was weird. What did he care about a football rally? I hoisted my gear bag strap on my shoulder and followed him.

Playing basketball again was a good thing. I missed playing with Reagan terribly, but I also felt most like myself during practice. At the end of a session, tired but loose from going all out, I almost felt relaxed. But then I would remember that my grades were making their way to my parents. And their history of thinking that schoolwork was more important than sports. And their benching Luke for better grades than mine.

Nothing relaxing about that.

And today my grades were headed for our mailbox. I held my gear bag tight like that would keep me on the court.

I was so worried about my parents' reaction that I barely heard anything during Spanish class. And I was still so frazzled that I walked into Kevin outside geometry.

"How's practice going?" he asked.

Surprised, I didn't reply. We weren't not talking, but the communication amounted to nods and one-liners after his fountain humiliation. "Awkward" was the operative word.

Kevin tried again. "When's the first game?"

"Next week," I said.

He smiled. "Does this mean we're talking?" he asked. "I mean we just exchanged a bunch of words."

"Possibly," I said.

"Probably?" he asked.

"Close enough," I said.

"Okay."

I didn't know what to do about Kevin, and I don't think he knew what to do about anything. He seemed more out of place than ever at school.

"We have that stupid pep rally this afternoon," he said.

What was the sudden interest in pep rallies?

"Yeah, basketball practice is delayed so they can put the bleachers back up," I said.

"Hard to believe those idiots made the conference finals."

I nodded.

"Last place I want to be," he said. "I might stay in the bathroom the whole time."

"Gross," I said. "Sit with me and we'll make faces at them."

He smiled.

"Or we can ignore them completely. Bring your drawings. I'd like to see your new stuff."

I had noticed he was sketching again.

"Okay."

At lunch, I thought about sneaking home and grabbing my report card from the mailbox. But Dad often drove to the house for a sandwich, and I didn't need to walk in on a tuna salad with a side of bad grades. And even if I beat him there and hid it, Luke's report card would beg the question about the location of mine.

I was doomed.

I headed to the gym for the pep rally, looking for Kevin on the way. I didn't see him, but he found me as I climbed the stands to sit with Maddie and Jonesy.

"Sam?" he called.

I motioned for him to join us.

"I thought you were on the outs," said Maddie.

I shrugged.

Kevin sat beside me and hissed when the football coach talked about perseverance and personal values.

"Doesn't he know who's playing for him?" he asked.

"Maybe he only knows them by number."

It got even more ridiculous. They had set up a big screen on the stage, and it displayed rolling photos from the season's games.

Kevin opened his sketchbook. He turned a few pages, and then he showed me scenes from the mini-golf farm.

"You went back?" I asked.

He blushed. "It was such a beautiful day when we played. I wanted to redo some of those sketches before all the leaves fell off."

I flipped through his drawings. Photographs couldn't capture the place any better.

"They are amazing," I said.

"And now celebrate your team!" announced the football coach, Coach Carter.

The football players appeared in the gym entrance, not only wearing the uniform jerseys they always wore on game days but wearing them over shoulder pads. It was like career day at elementary school.

The players lined up beside Coach Carter to a rising cheer from my fellow students. Anything was more fun than last-period classes.

Rocky Dent and Jim Dawson joined their teammates a few minutes late, with gray T-shirts over their shoulder pads. And two other players followed them, wearing the same garb.

Coach Carter looked at them curiously.

Rocky shrugged. He didn't know what happened to his jersey.

Students giggled. I went back to Kevin's drawings. I didn't care about their stupid uniforms.

But then the giggles grew into laughter, and then the laughter grew hysterical.

Kevin looked up. "No," he said. "I can't believe it."

The uniforms were found. Someone had hijacked the presentation, and the screen now showed the school fountain as viewed through a web cam. The missing uniforms lay in the water, weighted down with dumbbells, and a windup rubber duck wobbled in circles above them. The display was titled *Floating by Numbers*.

The "Rubber Duckie" song started to stream from the speakers.

Students sang along.

"Did you know about this?" asked Kevin.

Laughing, I shook my head. "It's awesome, though!"

Then I remembered that Luke had told me to pay attention.

Coach Carter stood with his mouth wide-open.

Hands on their hips, the football players searched the stands. It didn't dawn on me that they were looking for Kevin until Rocky spotted him and pointed.

"Oh no," said Kevin.

Rocky marched over to the stands and stood in front of our section.

"Are you kidding?" he yelled at Kevin, pointing to the screen.

"What?" replied Kevin.

"You know what!"

Kevin didn't know what. He shrugged.

Rocky didn't like that. He squeezed between sophomore girls sitting in front of us to get closer to Kevin.

"You fix this!" he yelled.

Kevin stood.

So did I. But I lost my balance in the tight quarters and started to fall.

Rocky grabbed my arm.

I didn't want his help. "Let go!" I said, and yanked his arm away.

And then I did fall.

"Get away from my sister!" yelled Luke, appearing out of nowhere. He lunged for Rocky and sent both of them tumbling over seated students.

"It's not your sister I want—it's him!" Rocky said, sitting on his landing bleacher and pointing at Kevin. "He dumped my jersey in the fountain!" He pointed at the screen. The rubber duck had slowed down, but it was still making eddies above the uniform jerseys on the bottom of the fountain.

"It wasn't him—it was me!" Luke yelled from where he had landed, a few bleachers below Rocky.

"What?" Rocky stood. "Why would you do that?"

"Why would you ruin someone's sketchbook?" asked Luke.

This was getting good.

"Who said I did that?" said Rocky with a smirk. He looked at Kevin. "But anyone who pushes me deserved it."

"Push like this?" asked Brain D. He pushed Rocky hard, and he fell into the sophomore girls, who screamed, which attracted the attention of the football players on the floor, who ran up to defend Rocky's honor. Which attracted the attention of Luke and Brain D.'s basketball teammates, who climbed over other sophomore girls to face off with the football team.

Except for the quarterback, Drew Carson, the principal's son, who, besides being well informed on the rules and potential punishments for creating a melee, also played basketball.

The football players and the basketball players faced off in the middle of the sophomore girls, trash-talking enough for a reality TV show. Kevin and I sat back down and watched like we had paid the price of admission.

I wondered what happened to the school security guard, but then Kevin poked me. The security guard was on the screen. He had decided to rescue the jerseys from the water, and his actions were caught on camera. The uniforms weren't important enough for wet shoes, and he stood in bare feet, with his pants rolled up to his knees, and reached for the final jersey. The rubber duck hit him in the shin.

"God, I hope that's being recorded," said Kevin.

"Any football player not on this floor by the time I count to ten will be suspended for the rest of the year," yelled Coach Carter into the microphone.

"One, two, three . . ." he yelled.

He looked at his players, who hadn't caught on yet.

"Four, five . . ."

Coach Harris grabbed the mike. "And that goes double for the basketball team. Six, seven, eight . . ." he said.

The basketball players scrambled down the bleachers, yelling, "Excuse me, excuse me."

The football players followed the basketball players. Rocky

slipped and launched himself into another group of girls. They screamed.

"Nine, nine and a half . . ." yelled Coach Harris.

Rocky jumped from the fourth bleacher to the gym floor. "Ten."

The football players stood next to Coach Carter, and the basketball players stood next to Coach Harris. They glared at one another, nostrils flaring like those of bulls facing their matador.

The security guard put one jersey over the webcam. It went dark.

Mr. Carson rushed to the microphone.

"The assembly is over," he said. "School is dismissed. See you at the game."

"Like hell," said Luke, standing close to the mic.

Everyone laughed.

Mr. Carson turned off the mic and yelled at my brother.

Kevin went outside with me while I waited for the gym to clear out for practice. We stood near the fountain and watched the floating rubber duck, which the security guard had left behind. Kids took selfies of themselves and the duck and the fountain.

"I still can't believe it," said Kevin. "I can't believe your brother did that."

"My guess is that Brain D. was in on it, too," I said. "And one of Luke's gaming friends. He's not great with computers."

Kevin shook his head. "I never thought I'd have that much fun in school."

I smiled. "You said you weren't supposed to be here. What did you mean?"

He stared at me. "You remembered."

I shrugged. "It struck me that I think about how Reagan is supposed to be here all the time, and you said that you weren't."

"I'm sorry," said Kevin. "I really don't mean to bring up sad memories."

"It's okay," I said. "But where were you going to school if not here? Bishop Hardy?"

He shook his head.

"There's this private school, in Massachusetts, that has an art program. My uncle was always going to send me. And I applied, and I got accepted and everything, but it didn't work out. My uncle's business tanked, and Dad and Mom didn't want to spend the college money they'd saved for that."

"Too bad," I said.

He nodded. "We fought about it," he said. "I wanted to go so bad, and I don't even know if I want to go to college."

"You must hate this place," said. "It's such a jock school."

"Hey, I play golf," he said.

"Did you go out for the golf team?"

"No."

We laughed.

"But I'd like to play with you again," he said. "If you want to."

"You asking for a rematch?"

"It only seems fair."

"Sure," I said.

Luke's coach called off practice so they could think about their actions, and so I got a ride home with him after mine finished. He and Brain D. were told that, since they were so keen to get the uniform jerseys wet, they could do the football team's wash after their final game. And they would also wash the basketball team uniforms that winter—Varsity and JV, girls and boys. We laughed about the pep rally all the way home, and we got hysterical at the idea of attending the football game and leading the crowd in a round of the "Rubber Duckie" song.

We walked into the kitchen to find Mom and Dad waiting at the table.

We stopped laughing.

"You guys, I don't know what Principal Carson told you, but it was just a prank and it was the reaction that started the riot, not the prank," said Luke.

"Prank?" asked Dad.

"Riot?" said Mom.

That's when I noticed the envelope in Dad's hand. And the official-looking letter under Mom's fingers.

They weren't waiting for Luke. My grades. How could I have forgotten?

"Shouldn't you be at practice?" Dad asked Luke.

"Uh," said Luke. "Coach called it off so we could think about the riot."

"I was really proud of Luke and Brain D.," I said. "The riot really wasn't their fault."

Dad looked at us like we couldn't be his children.

"Upstairs," Dad said to Luke. "And apparently, you're next."

Luke stomped up the stairs like he was Bradley.

"And you," said Dad. He pointed at my chair. "Sit."

I'm not sure whether it was the D-minus that most upset my parents, or the fact that not a single grade was above C.

"You got a C in gym," said Dad. "How is that even possible?"

"I can't explain that one," I said. "Except that we've played soccer all fall, and I really don't like soccer."

"You used to play soccer, for Pete's sake," said Dad.

"I know," I said. "So I kicked the ball to the other side regularly for the fun of it. I didn't know we were getting graded."

"I don't understand," said Mom. "I thought you were doing homework all that time in your room."

I shrugged. It wasn't going to help to tell them I had spent a certain amount of time in my room talking with Dead Reagan.

"Are you having trouble concentrating?" asked Dad.

"Is it taking you longer to comprehend your reading?" asked Mom.

I shook my head.

"Because well, that's part of feeling sad, and you are still grieving, and we would understand that," Mom said.

"And we can get you some help," said Dad.

I shook my head. "I don't really know," I said. "I haven't felt like doing any work."

My parents sat there, unsure of how to handle the "didn't feel like it" statement. That usually drove them mad.

"We made Luke quit his travel team when his grades were poor," Mom said.

"I remember," I said.

I sighed. I finally started to play ball again, and my parents were going to take it away. Nice job, I told myself. You just handed over the starting point guard position to Starr Regal. What a great going-away present for Reagan.

"But this is a different situation," said Mom.

"It is?" I didn't understand.

Dad nodded.

"It's a very different situation," said Mom.

I leaned closer.

"You're making progress," said Mom. "You're working out again, and you've started to play ball, and you're beginning to act like your old self." She hesitated. "I would imagine that playing ball without Reagan is difficult."

I nodded. "I think about her all the time when I'm on the court."

I didn't tell her that the gym was the one place that Dead Reagan avoided.

"I'm sorry it's so painful," said Mom.

"You are dealing with a terrible tragedy," said Dad.

"So," said Mom, "how about this? If you promise to work hard on your courses this quarter, you can keep playing basketball."

"And work hard means regardless of whether you feel like it," said Dad.

I could do that.

"I studied Spanish vocabulary last weekend. And I did a bunch of geometry assignments."

Mom slid her finger over the D-minus like an archaeologist touching an ancient artifact. "You seem to have a few more geometry assignments to go."

"Yes," I said.

"Are you working on vocabulary in English?" Dad asked. "A little practice for your PSATs and SATs?"

I nodded. "A little."

"I'll give you my cards," Dad said.

"Your what?"

"Flash cards from my day. It's a great way to learn new vocabulary. I'll find them and put them on your desk."

"Great. Thanks, Dad."

"Any questions?" asked Mom.

"No," I said. "But . . ."

"Yes?" said Dad.

"I'm really sorry," I said. "My grades. I'm sorry."

"We're not happy," said Dad. "But we understand how it could have happened."

Mom nodded. "But please keep us in the loop this time, okay? We are your parents after all."

"Okay," I said.

I couldn't believe they were letting me play. "Thanks."

"Now, would you mind getting your brother?" asked Dad.

UP ON THE ROOF

Samantha Wilson, serious student, walked into Carlow High Monday morning after the ultimate homework marathon weekend. I had even taken meals in my room except when Mom insisted I join everyone for Sunday dinner. I was up to November in geometry, and I had inhaled the Renaissance in world history. I just skimmed *The Red Pony* because I had already read it for the summer reading list and didn't like it. I studied Spanish vocabulary words for the upcoming week.

In school, I kept the momentum going. I put my hand up in geometry, much to Kevin's chagrin, and I worked an example at the board. I spent lunch reviewing my reading notes for English, and I sat down in world history with my timeline for the Age of Discovery.

When classes ended, I jogged onto the basketball court ten minutes early. I was ready and able to show Coach Collins that there was one and only one candidate for the point guard position—me.

I practiced jump shots.

Coach Gray walked in. "Just the person I needed to see," she said.

"Excuse me?" I stopped shooting.

"We need to talk," she said. "I'm the academic counselor for the winter sports teams."

Lord, I thought. Please don't tell me we're going to chat about my C in gym class.

"It's about your first-quarter grades," she said.

I braced for a conversation about not making a mockery of soccer—the beautiful game.

"We have a new rule here at Carlow High that says that freshmen with Ds can't play on a team until they get the D up to a C."

"What?" I held the ball tight.

"You have to improve your grades."

"I can't play basketball?"

"Right."

Unbelievable.

"But I'm eligible according to the state association rules." I had checked Brain D.'s version and he was spot on.

"Carlow High School has higher standards," she said.

I had myself a new nightmare.

"I can't play games?" I asked.

"You can't do anything—games or practice—until you get that D up to a C. In geometry, right?"

She took my complete paralysis as a yes.

"The idea is to give you time to focus on your academics. To give you the best possible chance for success in your new school. This policy is in your best interest."

Maybe I was supposed to be impressed by her command of school policy, but I was flabbergasted.

"I can't practice?"

"That's right. Just until you get that grade up with a few quizzes or a major test."

The paralysis returned.

"You've had a rough time," she said in a softer voice. "But that's even more of a reason to get you a better start with your academics."

"Okay." Although I wanted to say, "You clueless woman. Don't you know that I am doing the best I can, and even my demanding parents said I could keep playing basketball?"

Then again, I had neglected to tell my parents that most of my grades should have been Fs. I wouldn't have been eligible by anyone's rules if my teachers had been honest and didn't count showing signs of life as classroom participation. Mr. Pratt had been honest. That D-minus was the only grade I earned.

I walked away from Coach Gray, and then I ran out of the gym and hid in the cafeteria. When even the stragglers on the team should have made it to practice, I stole back into the locker room and stuffed my clothes into my gear bag. I put the half hearts around my neck before I headed out the back door and skulked all the way to the city library. I couldn't deal with questions from anyone, not even Bradley at home. I thumbed through issues of *Architectural Digest* in the magazine section because I was too upset to read words.

When I settled down, I pulled out my geometry notebook. The next test was over ten days away. No announced quizzes in sight. I didn't see myself talking Mr. Pratt into an earlier exam, although even he might appreciate the irony of the request.

Reagan caught up to me when I started to walk home.

"Girl, I had to put out an all-points bulletin to find you!"

I shrugged. "Don't you guys have GPS?"

"Local dead spot for interstellar networks," she replied. "What happened to practice?"

"I'm off the team," I said.

"What?"

"Temporarily, anyway. It turns out they have special rules at Carlow High. No Ds for freshman."

"Oh, crap," she said. "And after you killed yourself doing homework."

"I can't play until we have another geometry test," I said. "And I have to get a C. "

"Piece of cake," Reagan said.

I walked faster.

"Deep breaths," said Reagan. "No reason to give yourself a heart attack."

I shook my head. "You know, you could simply tell me that I'm feeling sorry for myself."

"What do you mean?"

"Killing myself? Heart attack? I get the message."

"That's not what I meant."

"Right."

I walked even faster. I wasn't feeling sorry for myself. I just needed a break.

"Sam, I'm the one feeling sorry for herself. I'm the one who can't believe what happened to me. I'm the one who's so jealous of you I could scream. I'm the one who still can't deal with a basketball court."

I stopped. Here I was, feeling sorry for myself for losing ten days of basketball when Reagan lost the rest of her life.

"You get a lousy C and you play again," she said.

The tears reappeared. "Oh, Reagan, I'm so sorry."

"I'm still facing up to the fact that I'm gone, too, you know."

Of course that hadn't crossed my mind. Of course I was so selfish that I didn't consider her fate.

We didn't talk for the next two blocks. I blinked back tears until my eyes hurt and I gave up and cried.

"Sam, don't."

"I'm surprised you're still here," I said.

"Come on," said Reagan. "Don't be silly."

I sniffled.

"Please stop."

That made me cry harder.

"I'll sing," Reagan said. "I'll make you feel better with a song."

"Please don't sing," I said between crying jags.

"Okay."

Instead, she started humming the melody to "Heart and Soul," the only duet we had mastered for the piano.

"Is that really appropriate?" I asked between whimpers.

"I need to face my demons."

"Oh God, this isn't one of those infamous Reagan 'Just Do It' moments, is it?"

She started singing "I Left My Heart in San Francisco."

"Really?"

She laughed. And then she immediately went into "Hungry Heart" by Bruce Springsteen, one of the songs Dad played on the only CD in his car.

It was hopeless. I sang along for a few bars.

"This is so morbid," I said. "Morbid and ghoulish."

"I define morbid," said Reagan. "I don't know about ghoulish."

And then she started singing "How Can You Mend a Broken Heart," by the Bee Gees, from a not-so-secret playlist of Mom's labeled MyOldSongs. Mom was still learning about sharing on a home network when we stumbled into it a couple years ago. Reagan loved the schmaltzy songs, and she knew all the words. She sang this one to the end, and I walked and listened. It was so sad.

We walked silently for several minutes. There was nothing to say about a girl who really had a broken heart. Who would never know about the other kind of broken heart. Who was being so brave about her broken heart.

"Hey, remember this one?" she asked.

Reagan started singing another one of Mom's songs, called "Heartbeat," by some old TV actor. We got hysterical when we first heard it—it was so silly that we invented a new category called "super pop" and we danced to it all around the house, mostly by hopping up and down to its incessant beat.

I laughed and hopped up and down as we made our way home.

Reagan giggled. "We never put together a cool playlist for your mom, did we?" she said.

"No." I kept hopping to the music on in my head.

"We were going to call it MyRealSongs, remember?"

I nodded.

"So she wouldn't be embarrassed if she was in an accident and someone looked through her phone apps."

"Like making sure you have clean underwear."

I assumed Reagan had clean underwear the day she died. Although it was probably soggy from playing basketball all afternoon.

I didn't need to think about that. I kept hopping.

"Maybe you could make your mom a decent playlist, anyway?" Reagan asked. "I really wanted to do that."

"I will," I said.

"Cool. Hey, I gotta run."

And she was gone.

Again.

A school bus rolled by too fast for me to stop hopping and

resume an age-appropriate pace. When it turned the corner, Maddie and Jonesy stared at me out of the back window of the Carlow High late bus.

Great.

I stopped hopping, but I kept thinking about Reagan's idea for the MyRealSongs playlist. Ideas had always popped out of her. I wondered if I'd ever had a single one of my own. I wondered if I had relied on Reagan for everything.

At home, I dropped my books on the side steps. I walked into the backyard and picked up Bradley's basketball. The grass looked like it could have used one more mowing before Dad put the lawn mower away for the winter, tucking it behind the plastic pool. The ladder leaned against the garage, where Luke had left it after cleaning the gutters over the weekend.

The trapeze at the circus popped into my head. And the time when Reagan and I had decided to invent our own daring circus act. We had put the plastic pool in the backyard, close to the garage, and filled it with pillows. Then we'd climbed onto the garage roof. We debated whether we could somersault together from the edge while holding basketballs and land safely in the pool. Dad came home early to find us standing up there.

"Girls!" he yelled. "What are you doing?"

He stepped to the ladder.

"Designing a circus act!" I said.

"Once we figure it out, we're going to charge kids to see it!" Reagan added.

"Wow," Dad said. "I can't wait to hear about it. But why

don't you come down and let's sketch it out in the kitchen?"

Dad was an engineer and had awesome graph paper.

"Okay," I said.

Dad held the ladder while we both climbed down the steps. We sat at the kitchen table for our planning conference. After an introduction to basic physics, we decided that the distance from the roof to the pool was too far for safety. We agreed that Mom didn't need to know anything about it, and we put the pillows back on their respective beds.

I stared at the garage roof. I couldn't remember who came up with the idea.

Still holding Bradley's basketball, I climbed the ladder. I stood on the roof. I couldn't believe Reagan and I had thought about jumping.

I closed my eyes, trying to remember who came up with the scheme.

Nothing. I stepped closer to the edge, and I tried to remember the pillow-filled pool sitting below. I closed my eyes again.

I was startled by the sound of a car door shutting.

"Sam, what are you doing on the roof? Get down this instant!"

"Mom?"

"Sam, we can talk when you get down," she said. She walked over and held the ladder. "We'll get you help—nothing is this bad!"

"Mom!" I said. "What do you think I was doing?"

"Please come down," she said.

"No," I answered. "I want to know."

"Sam, please come down. You're scaring me."

"God," I said. But I figured I better move.

"Here," I said. I tossed her the ball. She caught it and then dropped it.

I grabbed the top of the ladder and started scurrying down the steps.

"Careful, Sam," Mom said. "I don't want you flying off that thing."

I stopped on a middle rung. That was it. Reagan and I were going to call our act the Flying Dribble Queens. And I had invented the name, and I had come up with the whole idea myself. And Reagan had been the one who insisted we plan it right away, and she was the reason Dad found us on the roof.

We had been a great team, Reagan and me. But I wasn't just along for the ride. I did my share.

"Would you please get down now?" Mom said.

"Sure, Mom," I said. "I'm coming."

She grabbed my arm when I reached the ground and hugged me. Then she wheeled me onto the back porch.

"Mom," I said. "It's not what you think."

"Right. You decided to stand on the edge of the garage roof because it was such a pretty day."

"Kind of," I said.

"On the same afternoon that Maddie and Jonesy saw you acting weird on the way home from school after you skipped practice!"

I cringed. "So that's why you came home early?"

"This isn't about me," she said. "Start talking."

I sat in the lawn chair. I took a deep breath to enjoy feeling better about myself before I dealt with Mom's fear that I was insane and/or suicidal.

"What do you want to know first?" I asked. "What the spies on the bus saw or what you saw driving up when you should have been working?"

"Sam."

I stretched my legs. "You want me to choose?"

She pulled the chaise lounge closer and sat. She leaned forward. "Start talking."

Since explaining why Dead Reagan and I were dancing to a song on her old playlist seemed harder, I went with the depressed daughter standing on the roof.

"I was trying to remember something that Reagan and I did a long time ago. It was a dumb idea, and Dad talked us out of it."

She narrowed her eyes. "I don't remember any story about you two being on the roof."

"We didn't tell you," I said. "And neither did Dad."

"You want me to believe that Dad didn't tell me about two children putting themselves in danger by climbing on the roof?"

"Dad doesn't tell you everything," I said.

"We'll see about that," she said.

I hoped the donuts weren't at risk.

"And the hopping around on the sidewalk?" she asked.

"So what, do Jonesy and Maddie videotape me?" I asked. "That's a violation of my privacy."

"Don't try to distract me."

"Yes," I said. "I was hopping."

Mom stared. "Could you use some more words?"

"Do you know about plyometrics?" I asked.

She narrowed her eyes.

"Well, I'm getting excited about basketball again and I was visualizing training drills and, well, I got carried away."

I didn't look at her, but I could feel Mom's incredulous stare. It was the same stare I got when we both knew the reason for the kitchen being spotless sometimes had nothing to do with my help-with-the-housework explanation and everything to do with an unapproved baking project that went wrong.

She sighed. "I don't believe you." She grabbed my knee. "And I thought you promised to keep us in the loop."

"I did."

"So when were you going to tell me about skipping practice?"

I told her about the Carlow freshman rule.

BACKSEAT DRIVER

Saturday morning, Mom looked up from her paper.

Luke, Bradley, and I concentrated on our cereal boxes.

"You people look pathetic," she said.

"We'd have more pep if Dad could still get donuts," Luke said.

"He's not allowed," replied Mom.

Dad held out his hands, palms up, like he had tried.

"I keep reading the ingredients of these wheat things, and there's nothing in them to wake you up," Luke said.

Mom had bought a variety of good-for-you cereal since we'd complained so much about having the sugary ones thrown out. So far, we hadn't tasted any we could stand.

Good thing I wasn't hungry.

Although I should have been starved. I didn't eat in the school cafeteria all week, not wanting to hear about basketball from Maddie and Jonesy. I made up excuses about needing to study in the library. The first couple of days, they had texted me about how much they needed me back because Starr made so many mistakes playing point. But those texts had stopped by the end of the week, and I worried that Starr was doing just fine.

Bradley grimaced but finished off his bowl of pretend Lucky Charms. "I'm done," he said. "I'm going to Tim's house, okay?"

He was already dressed. Mom hadn't yet figured out the routine. Bradley rushed to Tim's as soon as possible on Saturday mornings before their chocolate-chip bagels ran out.

"Sam, it's time to teach you how to drive," announced Dad.

"What?" I asked.

"She gets thrown off the basketball team and she gets to drive?" asked Luke.

Dad frowned. "Apologize right now."

Mom gave Luke a dirty look, too. She and Dad were not happy about the freshman sports rule. They wanted to talk with Principal Carson about an exception due to my circumstances, but I didn't let them. I was sick of being special.

"I'm sorry, Sam," Luke said.

His remorse lasted five seconds. Then he sat up straight. "But she's only fourteen." He snorted. "I was fifteen before you took me out driving."

"I'm fifteen in six months," I said.

"And you're a boy and she's a girl," Dad said. He was ready for action with his weekend jeans and faded UNH sweatshirt.

"Unbelievable," said Luke.

I smiled at Dad. He smiled at Mom.

Then he nodded his head at the door. "Throw on some clothes and I'll meet you at the car."

"Sure," I said. I headed upstairs.

Dad started the car when I opened the back door. I guessed the lesson wouldn't begin in the driveway.

"We're going to the Mill Town warehouse parking lot," he said when I climbed in the car. "It's empty on the weekends."

But he drove toward Main Street.

"Dad?"

"We have an errand to run first."

"An errand or Polly's?"

He shrugged.

A few minutes later, Dad and I sat in Polly's parking lot, eating chocolate-covered raised donuts with sprinkles.

"So, the driving lesson was a ruse?" I asked.

Dad shook his head. "Oh no, we're definitely on."

"Cool," I said.

Dad drove north on Main Street, sipping coffee and listening to his Bruce Springsteen CD. He drove way past the country club road and pulled into Mill Town, tapping his fingers to "Born to Run." He stopped in the dead center of the parking lot.

"Okay," he said. "Switch sides."

In a few seconds, I fastened the driver's seat belt.

"Now what?" I asked.

Dad looked at me oddly. "You know, start up the car."

I shrugged. "How?"

"You're kidding, right?"

"No," I said, beginning to feel stupid.

"You don't know how to start a car?"

"If I knew how to drive, I wouldn't need you to teach me!" I said loudly.

"Hey," said Dad. "That's okay. I was just surprised."

My eyes got misty.

"Really!" said Dad. "Luke thought he knew everything." He laughed. "So he didn't listen. I'm surprised the car survived our first time out."

I nodded.

"Really, this is better," Dad said. "I get to teach you everything the right way."

I nodded again. But I realized this was yet another thing I had counted on Reagan to do. She was four months older than me, so she would have learned to drive first and then helped me. I wondered if I'd ever done anything by myself.

"Sam?" Dad said. "You ready? If not, we can always try again next week."

"No," I said. "I want to start today."

"Good," he said. "Because it's a beautiful day for driver's ed."

He rolled up his sleeves. "Watch me."

He checked to see that the car was in Park, pushed the Start button, and the engine cranked up.

"Now, things will be different once your mother talks me into that electric car, but we'll deal with that later, okay?"

I laughed.

He shut off the engine. "Now you."

Within five minutes, I drove the Subaru around the Mill Town parking lot. It felt great. I did circles around the lot like I used to do circles in the driveway with my tricycle.

"Whee!" I said.

Dad cracked up. "It's fun, isn't it?"

I braked to a smooth stop. "It's fantastic!"

Dad made me practice more stopping after that, and I even got to brake so hard that I left skid marks on the parking lot. We got out of the car to check them out.

"That's laying down some rubber," Dad said.

"You told me to do it!" I said.

"That's right," he said. "You need to know how your car reacts to slamming on the brakes."

I nodded.

"And then you hope you never have to do that on the road." He hesitated. "But you will. It always happens."

He leaned against the car.

"I'll be a safe driver, Dad," I said. "I promise."

"I hope so," he said.

But he had the same look that came over Mom sometimes when I knew she was thinking about Reagan. It was the look that said that she could lose a child, too. And it was the worst look I had ever seen on either one of them.

Except the day Mom told me Reagan was dead.

I took a deep breath. And I leaned against the car like

Dad and let the sun try to warm up the chilly November day. It was completely silent except for the hum of the interstate miles away.

"Time for the real road," Dad said.

"What? Don't I need a driver's permit for that?"

Dad got the look he got when he listened to a bunch of Springsteen. "Let's be rebels," he said. "We're born to run."

I laughed.

"I'm not taking you on the highway," he said. "Just out here. The roads are nearly empty."

"I don't know, Dad," I said. "First time out?"

"Yes, I'm supposed to have you practice in a parking lot endlessly before I take you on the road, but you're doing great. You're ready for the next step."

"Really?"

"Sam, you'll be doing exactly the same thing you've done here for the last hour. Foot on the gas, stop, turn, foot on the gas."

It had been pretty straightforward. And I was feeling confident.

"Okay."

I drove to the exit. I stopped at the road, and I looked both ways about a dozen times. Then I turned right and managed to stay between the lines all the way to the stop sign.

"Now, always come to a complete stop," he said. "That's an important habit to establish."

I kept my foot on the brake.

"No rolling stops, ever," he said. "Eventually they get you into trouble."

"Okay," I said. "Rolling stops. Negative."

I signaled for a right-hand turn.

"Nice," said Dad. "Again, always signaling is a good habit."

I drove around the Mill Town block four more times. Dad would have been content to do that the entire day, as long as he could keep playing his Springsteen CD.

Me. Sam. Driving.

"There's a drive-in out here," he said. "Great burgers."

"Grass-fed beef?" I asked. "Mom would want to know."

"Let's assume," he said.

"Should I pull over so you can drive?" I asked.

"Nope," he said. "You're doing fine."

"Keep going?" I asked.

"Yes," he said. "And then take a right on Mansfield Road."

A car headed our way. It was my first other car and I tensed up.

"You're fine," said Dad. "Just keep the car in its lane."

The other car, a red Ford something, zipped by.

"He's going too fast," I said.

Dad laughed.

There was no more traffic before I reached the intersection with Mansfield. I stopped, signaled, and waited for a car to pass before I turned onto it.

"Done like a pro," Dad said.

"Look at you," Reagan said from the back seat.

I nodded slightly.

"This is, like, amazing," she said.

It sure was.

"Don't mind me," Reagan said. "I'm going to sit back and enjoy the ride."

"Check your seat belt," I told her.

"Ah, seat belt's fine," Dad said. "But thanks for asking."

Whoops. My face reddened.

Reagan giggled.

A couple of miles later, Dan's Drive-In showed up on the right-hand side, next to a pasture with a dozen cows. The small dirt parking lot held three cars.

"Dad," I said, panicking. "We haven't practiced parking."

"No problem," he said. "Slow down and turn in."

I did. I stopped when I was off the road.

"And drive over to the right."

I did.

"And pull in here." He pointed to a Dumpster. "Just don't hit the Dumpster and you're perfect."

I gave the Dumpster twenty feet, and I parked.

"Perfect," said Dad.

I smiled. "Better than Luke?"

"You didn't hit anything, did you?"

I laughed.

"Come on," Dad said. "Let's have lunch and celebrate."

"I would kill for a cheeseburger," Reagan said from the back seat.

I would kill to get you one, I thought.

YOUR CHEATING HEART

I felt better about everything after my driving lesson. In fact, I felt good enough to take Bradley to the Saturday-afternoon movie downtown. After Dad dropped us off, I waited in the lobby while Bradley treated himself to a big tub of popcorn and a supersized drink.

Horror flicks were my secret vice. A scary movie could keep me planted in a movie seat.

"Carry this," said Bradley, handing me the popcorn.

"I don't think I can carry anything that big," I said.

"Very funny."

Inside Cinema Two, we settled in the back row and worked on the popcorn as the movie began. I elbowed Bradley a few times when the Coke slurping got out of control, but I understood his excitement with junk food. And what happened in the downtown theater stayed in the downtown theater.

The movie was good, and I felt relaxed when it ended and we headed outside, despite the multiple strangulations and stabbings.

And then I saw Kevin on the sidewalk. With a redheaded girl. Heads together. Laughing. No doubt entertained by the same movie.

Entertained together.

I stopped short, and Bradley ran into me.

"Hey, why did you stop?" asked Bradley.

"Why don't you look where you're going?" I said.

Kevin and the girl disappeared around the corner.

"Come on," I told Bradley. We walked home in record time.

Luke was shooting baskets when we reached the house. He threw the ball at me.

I threw it back.

"The idea is to throw it at the basket," he said. "It's called practice."

"I'm not allowed," I said.

I hadn't touched a ball since Coach Gray kicked me out of the gym last Monday.

"That attitude will get you everywhere," he said.

"I'll practice," said Bradley.

"I'm mad at you," Luke told him.

Bradley looked confused. "I got two As and two Bs."

Luke laughed.

I didn't.

"I'm mad at you because you keep grinding dirt into your jeans," he said. "I can't get the stains out."

I grinned. Luke's punishment for tossing the football jerseys into the fountain was doing all the laundry at home, too.

"I'm just playing outside like regular," said Bradley. "Sometimes the ground is muddy."

"Well, play smarter," said Luke. "I can't spend all my time presoaking your stupid clothes. I barely have time for homework now."

"Yes, sir," said Bradley.

Luke fired the ball at me again.

I threw it back harder.

"Seriously, Sam," he said. "Unless you're quitting this team, too."

"I didn't quit," I said. "I got kicked off."

Luke dribbled the ball. "Temporarily. And it's not the first time it's happened. Just ace your geometry test and you're good."

I shook my head. "And then I get to watch Starr Regal run the team?"

"So that's it," he said. He picked up his dribble. "Jealous?"

"No," I said.

"Then what?"

"It's not supposed to be this way," I said.

Luke frowned. He bounced the ball. "Yeah."

"I don't know what to do," I said.

Luke pounded the ball into the driveway. Then he held it. "Maybe just play?" he said.

He passed me the ball. "Didn't Reagan always say, 'Practice. It's everything'?"

I nodded—Reagan and her sayings.

Luke chuckled. "Just do it."

I smiled. "How do you know all her lines?"

"Reagan practically lived here," said Luke.

True. I hugged the ball. "I miss her," I said.

"Me too," said Luke. "I really miss her, too."

I bounced the ball. Luke was right. I needed to deal with the here and now and the fact that I would be back on the team. I had studied so much geometry that I was seeing triangles and circles everywhere.

"Catch me up?" I asked.

"Sure," said Luke.

I remembered that Reagan was going to make "Just Eat It" the motto of her Dribble Queen ice-cream chain.

"Then can we go to Dairy Queen?"

"Before supper?"

"Exactly," I said.

"You're on!"

Luke stationed himself under the basket. I made six baskets in a row.

"When's your test?" he asked.

"Next week," I said.

"Perfect," said Luke. "What day?"

"Wednesday."

"You'll be on the team on Thursday."

"I hope so," I said. I made another three baskets.

"Brain D. said he'd help you study if you wanted."

I laughed. "Isn't senior year late for geometry?"

"They had some glitch with the grading system and it turns out he didn't pass it by the skin of his teeth his sophomore year. He failed it by the skin of his teeth."

"You're kidding," I said. "Doesn't he get a gimme or something?"

"Nope. Carlow High takes its standards very seriously."

"So I'm told," I said.

"He has to take it again to graduate."

Talking about geometry made me think of Kevin. We were just friends, and I had made a fine art of pushing him away, but the image of him with that other girl was infuriating. I missed the next shot.

Luke rebounded a couple sets of foul shots for me, and then we hopped into his truck to ride to the Dairy Queen. Fueled by a hot-fudge sundae, I spent another hour studying circles—angles and radii and chords, oh my—until I knew it cold. I don't know whether opening the book was the key or if my brain was waking up, but something was working. I closed the book. One test, one C or better, and I was home free.

Sam-I-am was coming back.

———————————

I turned into Elliot Park on Sunday morning. I hadn't run for days, and I was feeling it. December was around the corner, and the cold made my rusty body feel worse. My ears were freezing, too, and I wished I had pulled on my wool cap. I headed for the duck pond.

"How's the weekend going?" asked Reagan.

"I've had better ones," I said.

"At least the movie was good."

"You were there?" I asked. "You should have said something."

"You know I hate talking in the movies."

"Very funny," I said. I sped up.

"Whoa, give me a little warning," Reagan called from behind me.

I slowed down. "Can you believe Kevin?"

"What do you mean?" asked Reagan.

"Maybe you missed it. He was there, too, with some girl."

"I was watching the movie."

"Outside afterward."

"You mean when I was reading the credits?"

"That was always so annoying."

"So?" asked Reagan.

"So he was there with some redheaded girl."

"And?"

"Well, you know," I said.

"I keep telling you, I can't read your mind."

"You used to."

"Things are different now."

"You're telling me."

"Well, he could have asked me to go to the movies with him."

"Really?" asked Reagan.

"What do you mean?"

"Well, you've run away from both golf dates," Reagan

said. "Maybe having you do that during a movie wasn't so appealing."

"Very funny."

"Besides, when did he become your boyfriend?"

"He's not," I said. "We're just friends."

"So why don't you tell your friend you saw him at the movies?"

"I don't want to know about his date."

"You already do," Reagan said. "If it was a date."

"What else could it be?"

"Why don't you find out?"

"Maybe I don't want to know."

Reagan sighed. "You want to know so bad it's killing you."

My legs were warming up. I started another loop around the duck pond. If it stayed cold like this, we'd be skating on it before Christmas. I nearly tripped over a castaway mitten.

"Stop thinking about skating and start thinking about basketball," said Reagan.

"I thought you couldn't read my mind."

"It's more like watching a movie for the hundredth time," said Reagan. "You get cold, you see the pond, and you think about skating. It happens every year."

"Sorry to be so predictable."

"It's endearing," said Reagan. "Now, speaking of basketball, you realize you have a game next Friday."

"I'm not on the team, remember?"

"Minor issue," said Reagan. "Ace the test on Wednesday, practice Thursday, and play in Friday's game."

"I seriously doubt Coach Collins will see it that way. I'll have to earn my way back."

"Isn't learning earning?" asked Reagan. "Isn't that enough?"

"What a comedian," I said.

I started another loop around the pond. I was tired, but I had to work on fitness.

"You're crazy," said Reagan. "You're on your own."

I nodded and kept going.

————————————

"You ready?" Luke asked when we'd finished lunch on Sunday and cleared the table.

"Ready for what?"

"Reviewing your team's plays," he said.

I didn't get it.

Luke held up one, two, and then three fingers.

"What is this? Charades?" I asked.

Luke rolled his eyes. "Remember? Basketball games? Plays?"

"Right," I said. "You run plays in basketball games."

"No, you idiot. Your plays. I watched your practices last week between wash cycles."

"Really?"

Luke picked up a pad of paper and pen from the counter.

"Sit," he said.

KNOWING ALL THE ANGLES

I finished my geometry test early. I passed it in and reviewed my notes for an upcoming English quiz. Samantha Wilson—study machine. I wondered how many students at Carlow had climbed from Cs and a D to honor roll in one quarter, because that's what I planned to do. On the way out, I passed Coach Gray in the doorway. She winked and pointed at the cell phone in her hand.

I got it. I should check my phone before I left school for the day. I wondered how Mr. Pratt would feel about on-demand grading. Just in case, I had brought my gear bag.

Kevin tapped me on my arm. "How did you do?"

"Good, I think."

"It was harder than usual," he said.

"Really?"

Kevin grinned. He knew about my situation.

"Do you think Pratt found out about me?"

"Absolutely."

"Well, he'd have to try harder than that," I said.

"Excellent," said Kevin.

My phone vibrated during lunch, which I was spending in an empty classroom, learning more about Finny than Gene ever knew. Sure enough, Coach Gray had sent an email congratulating me on regaining my status with the team. I leaped out of my seat like a cheerleader. Yes!

I sprinted to the locker room at the final bell, and I was dressed and heading out as my teammates arrived. In the empty gym, Coach Gray practiced her jump shot, which needed practice.

"Ready?" she asked.

I nodded. "Thanks," I said. "For getting my test graded so fast."

"Being an academic counselor has its power," she said. "We want progress, not retribution. And lucky for you, you had a test fairly soon."

"I was surprised Mr. Pratt graded it so quickly," I said.

"Oh, it wasn't his choice," she said. "Something about doing it in the privacy of his home."

I figured the retribution would come later.

"But the rules are the rules. Lucky for you, he has a study period right after your class."

"What did I get?"

"A-minus."

I couldn't help smiling. "I'll take it."

"By the way, the other grades didn't look so good," she said. "Are his tests always so hard?"

I shrugged.

Coach Gray handed me the ball, and we shot around as the other players came on the floor and warmed up. The noise level grew with more dribbling balls, shots thudding against the backboards, and incessant chatter.

Coach Collins walked in last and looked surprised to see me. He put out his hand. "Good work," he said.

"Thank you, Coach."

"Nice to have you back," he said. "But you'll have to catch up, you know."

"I don't expect to play on Friday," I said.

He nodded. "You won't start," he said. "But you'll dress out." He smiled.

I was secretly relieved about not starting. The whole point of playing was so that no one would take Reagan's place except me. But taking the place of Reagan and Sam without Reagan was starting to worry me.

In fact, it was overwhelming.

But then I looked at the stage at the far end of the gym, and I thought about riding past the building all summer and Reagan proclaiming that this gym would be our stage. I couldn't let her down. I had to play so well that it would be like Reagan was playing, too.

After some defensive positioning drills and conditioning drills that lasted way too long, Coach Collins turned to scrimmaging. He put me on the subs squad. But I knew the plays cold, so I blocked the very first pass that Starr attempted—she was still thinking her way through and telescoped it. I recognized the next play, too. I anticipated Starr's pass underneath and moved Jonesy in place with a quick head nod. She collected that ball and hit me with a downcourt lob for the breakaway basket.

"Nice," said Coach Collins when we stopped. "It's like you haven't missed a thing."

I grinned. "Thanks, Coach," I said.

Thanks, Luke, I thought.

After another fifteen minutes of structured scrimmaging, with Coach Collins interrupting play for teachable moments, he whistled for a break. I grabbed a long drink at the water fountain. Then I stretched my quads, holding each ankle in turn.

Sandy stood beside me, wiping off sweat with a towel. "I think he wants to put you in for Starr."

"I missed a week of practice," I said, not knowing who knew what about my grades.

"And Coach has his rules," she said.

"Starr isn't bad."

"Not bad at all," she said. "But I like you at point."

Coach Gray blew her whistle. "Back to it," she yelled.

Coach Collins kept me on the subs squad the whole time, and I haunted Starr Regal on defense. At first, she was irritated, but she toughened up once she knew I played for keeps. She protected the ball well, and I only poked it away a couple more times.

I did push her buttons a few times with some touch fouls.

"Wilson," Coach Gray called once when Starr pulled up

from dribbling and stared me down. "It's not an actual game."

"No, no," said Coach Collins. "Good play, Wilson, keep on. Game conditions, that's what we want."

He shot Coach Gray a look that said I don't know what you guys do in soccer practice, but we practice for keeps in the gym.

So Starr put the ball on the floor and I kept pushing her and she definitely dealt with it. I guarded into the range of callable fouls, but it didn't faze her. Maybe the California mind-set wasn't such a bad thing on the basketball court. She clearly wasn't my defensive match when we went the other way, though, and I took advantage of her overguarding me two times in a row to cut loose for easy jumpers.

"Enough!" she screamed the second time.

I could only grin.

"Nice work, Wilson," Coach Gray yelled from the sidelines.

When practice ended, we walked out of the gym past the varsity guys waiting in the hallway.

"Look at my hands!" I heard Luke tell another player. "They're chapped from scrubbing those stupid football uniforms."

I stood outside the gym door and watched the first ten minutes of the boys' practice. After a couple of laps around the floor, they began boxing out drills, their big weakness from last season. Boxing out was basic technique, and Reagan used to mutter at their mistakes at the games. Luke played small forward sometimes, and I winced when their big center, Matt Bonet, hammered him. He would feel that tomorrow.

By the time I walked into the locker room, it was deserted. And that felt strange. And I realized that's because Reagan was usually with me.

I stood still and breathed in and out, listening to the sounds of the heating pipes and the whistle from the boys' practice. A toilet gurgled. A long-ago poster of Mia Hamm was taped to the wall next to a corkboard with inspirational quotes written on index cards. I hadn't noticed them before. I wondered if I was so caught up with Reagan that I stopped noticing what was going on around me.

Outside, I debated whether to call home for a ride or battle the chill and wind, courtesy of a new cold front. I decided on arctic character building, although I wished I had brought sweatpants by the time I cut across the parking lot and walked by the school entrance.

"Geez, it's cold," said Reagan.

"You're not the one with bare legs," I said.

"How do you know?"

"Good point," I said.

"Good practice," she said.

"You watched? I thought it was too hard for you."

"Just the last fifteen minutes," she said.

I didn't know what to say.

"That's why I'm so cold!" she said. "Stood out here for an hour getting up my nerve."

I still didn't know what to say. I wasn't trying to make Dead Reagan's life harder.

"And?" I finally said.

"And it was okay," she said. "After the first few minutes. And watching both Maddie and Jonesy run into you on the subs squad was worth it!"

"Putting me on the subs team wasn't necessary," I said.

"Well," Reagan said.

"I did my work," I said. "I aced that test."

"After months of no work," said Reagan

"Mr. Pratt was not happy about the forced grading," I said.

"I'll bet."

"He'll get back at me, I know it."

"Just keep studying. Pratt has no power if you've got grades."

The wind grew stronger, and I zipped up my jacket.

"Starr isn't bad," I said. "Although she's a lot easier to defend than you."

"Goes without saying."

"Humility is intact, I see."

"Are you excited about the game?" she asked.

I shrugged. "I don't know how much Coach Collins will play me."

"He better play you a lot," said Reagan. "I'm coming."

"Really?" I said.

"It's time," she said. "I watched you guys today, and I didn't melt or anything."

"That would be great," I said.

"Hey!"

I turned around. Kevin stood at the front entrance, and he put his index finger up, like he'd wait for me.

Wait for me to do what? I thought.

"Your fella's calling you," said Reagan. "I'll see you later."

I walked over to Kevin.

"Hey, you got some Bluetooth going on?" he asked.

"No," I said.

"But I heard you talking to someone," he said.

"Oh," I said. "Right, Bluetooth."

He looked at me like something was going on and it wasn't Bluetooth.

"What are you still doing here?" I asked. "Don't tell me you've picked up an after-school activity."

He shook his head. "Mr. Pratt," he said. "Making a paper airplane from the preview sticky is a punishable offense."

"That was weeks ago."

"He has an excellent memory."

"That stinks."

"You got a ride coming?" I asked.

"Yeah, my dad's picking me up," he said. "You want one?"

"Sure," I said, shivering. I rubbed my arms. "Hey, what do they think of all the detentions?" I asked.

"What detentions?" he said, smiling.

"Don't they send reports to your parents?"

"Not if I gave them an email address that goes to me," he said.

"Nice." I laughed. "So how is the Holt boy doing?"

"Four As, except for a C in geometry, and seventeen detentions."

"And the parental feedback?"

"Very disappointed with his geometry grade. But sure that Kevin will try harder."

We both laughed.

"I won't tell you what I got in geometry, but you did better," I said.

He shook his head.

Reagan was right. I should just ask Kevin about his date.

"So did you guys like the movie on Saturday?"

Kevin looked surprised. "You mean the slasher matinee?"

I nodded. "I saw you there."

"It was okay," he said. "Well, actually my cousin thought it was dumb, but I thought it was good."

Cousin.

"I didn't know you had a cousin."

I couldn't help smiling.

"Yeah, she lives in Mansfield. Sometimes she and her mom come up to visit and we ditch the parents and go to the movies."

I was still stuck on "cousin."

A black SUV drove up.

"That's our ride," said Kevin. He opened the front passenger door. "Dad, can we take Sam home first?"

Still smiling, I got into the back seat.

NOW YOU SEE ME, NOW YOU DON'T

I didn't miss a shot in practice on Thursday, but Coach Collins kept me on the subs squad. I know he wanted to see what Starr and I could do together, but he had to make the point that he wouldn't tolerate academic slips. Dead friend or not.

And so I sat on the bench Friday night. The last time I had started on my butt, I was eleven and nursing a sprained ankle. You weren't allowed to suit up if you couldn't play, so I had sat there with my crutches, my air cast, and my uniform underneath my street clothes.

Waiting for the referee to toss the jump ball in our home gym, I fidgeted worse than Nathan Hamill. I clasped my hands over my head to keep from launching out of my seat.

We won the tip-off. Within seconds, Starr launched a bomb from the top of the key. Coach Collins bolted up in frustration. Then the shot fell though the nets, and he raised his fist in celebration. He wanted Starr to work the ball like he instructed, but he also liked points.

Maddie poked me. "He's going to have fun with her."

"Oh, yeah," I replied.

After Mansfield missed their first shot and Sandy rebounded it, Starr took one look at Coach Collins and figured she better stick to the game plan. She held up one finger and ran the motion offense. We didn't make the shot, but Coach Collins nodded his head at the execution.

We got into a rhythm of making baskets and having Mansfield answer them, and you got the feeling the game would hit barn-burner territory. I stretched my ankles and arms periodically to make sure I was ready for action.

Prisha gave the tired signal halfway through the first quarter. Coach Collins reached over and tapped me on the shoulder. Kneeling at the scorer's table, I felt a swoosh of anxiety, and I looked at the stands for support. I found Mom and Dad near the centerline. And I spotted Luke and Brain D. in the student section. Luke saw me and raised both fists.

The butterflies disappeared when I stepped on the floor. Starr nearly knocked me down with a behind-the-back pass on a play designed to go to cutters under the basket. Luke had taught me the plays better than Coach Collins had taught Starr.

She tried it again after Mansfield scored. I had a feeling it was coming, even though Coach Collins yelled, "Cutters, cutters," when she dribbled the ball down the court. Maybe she forgot what cutters did. I grabbed her pass, dribbled a few times, found Sandy faithfully running her cuts, and nailed her. Sandy turned and made a quick layup.

"That's how you do it," yelled Reagan.

She was there. I was psyched.

"Looking good," she yelled.

That was so loud that I figured everyone heard it. But no, when I looked around, no one seemed concerned about hearing a dead girl's voice.

I smiled.

Mansfield went on a scoring binge after that, beating our press consistently to tie the game at 18–18.

Coach Collins grew frustrated. "The press is just hustle," he yelled. "But you have to hustle!"

Despite his concerns, I felt good. I loved playing in games— the crowd noise, the referee's whistle, the squeaking shoes, and the ball smacking the floor.

We took the ball up the court to find Mansfield in a zone defense.

"Three, Starr, three," yelled Coach Collins, and held up three fingers.

Starr held up three fingers, too. Then she dribbled in place at the top of the key. The three play meant shifting attention to the far side and then swinging the ball back to me, with a screen set by Sandy. And Starr did exactly that, passing back and forth with Maddie a few times and then whipping the ball to me, standing left of the free-throw line. Sandy gave me all the time in the world to launch my trademark jumper.

"The ball. Is in. The hoop," yelled Reagan.

The ball swished through the net.

Yes!

As I backpedaled to defense, I noticed Kevin sitting on the top bleacher. Cool.

Prisha replaced me, and Coach Collins high-fived me when I sat down.

I gulped from a paper cup of water. "Think, Starr!" I yelled.

The game was tied at halftime. In the locker room, Coach Collins reminded us of the running we had agreed to do on our own, and he promised to supplement it with a special set of suicide drills next week.

"No one beats our press that easily!" he yelled.

My teammates shifted uncomfortably.

"And, Starr," he said, "we only have three plays, right? And none of them include throwing the ball at the basket from midcourt!"

California girl nodded.

We ran back onto the court when the buzzer sounded for the second half, and I do mean ran.

Prisha stayed in the game. I threw my warm-up jacket around my shoulders.

We played well. We seemed energized, and Starr stuck with Coach's plan. I won't say that everyone had the plays memorized, but there were periods of execution that made us look like we had played together for months.

I substituted for Prisha again, and I didn't take any shots, but I did knock the ball away from my player as Mansfield took the ball up the court. I retrieved it and threw a baseball pass to the breaking Starr for an assist.

We were down 47–45 when we began the final quarter. Starr ran the motion offense and took advantage of an opening in the middle to drive to the basket. She collided with a huge Mansfield player who stepped in front of her. Starr crumpled to the floor.

The referee blew her whistle. Foul on Mansfield.

Starr didn't get up. She held her ankle. By the look on her face, her feet would not be dancing anytime soon.

"Coach?" yelled the second referee, squatting to look at Starr's foot.

Coach Collins and Coach Gray helped Starr hobble off the floor. After they settled her on the bench, Coach Collins pointed at me. "Wilson," he said. "In for Starr."

I jumped up and ran to the scorer's table.

A tsunami of anxiety hit me this time. I felt like puking. I was getting the point position, exactly what I wanted, and I was terrified.

I wasn't ready to take charge. I hadn't played serious minutes there for years. Reagan had become the point guard, and I had become the scoring machine. I didn't know why I thought I could play point in a real game now. Where was Lilly Myers when I needed her?

I grabbed the half hearts and tried to settle down.

The scorer hit the buzzer. I was in. I took a long breath. I was being ridiculous. If there was anything I knew how to do, it was play basketball. I could play any position, and I could play it well. I walked to the foul line. I didn't think or hesitate or even stretch. I simply made both of Starr's free throws to tie the game.

And I didn't do any more thinking when I found my man on defense. Their point guard was shorter than me, and she could only move right. So I jammed her, and she lost the ball out of bounds right after she caught a pass.

But when Sandy tossed me the ball from the sidelines, my autopilot stopped, and I started thinking again.

And you only get in trouble in sports when you do that.

I thought about how it was on me to play well in honor of Reagan. And that made me think of how unfair it was to be playing without Reagan. I choked up. When I dribbled down the court to begin our offense, I dabbed tears out of my eye with my free hand.

I stood at the top of the key and bounced the ball. I licked my lips. I couldn't decide what play to call. I slowed my dribble to Reagan style: Bounce, two, three. Bounce, two, three.

It didn't help.

Finally, Coach Collins bellowed, "Two! Two!"

I held up two fingers and threw the ball to Sandy, who had come up to post on the left side. She turned and found herself covered. Then she whipped it to Prisha, who'd drifted to the baseline, and she sank the twelve-foot jumper.

I hustled back on defense, sweating way more than my minutes warranted. Mansfield missed an easy jump shot, and Jonesy tossed me the rebound.

I slowed it down on the way to the other end. While my teammates got into their offensive set, I told myself to pretend it was old times, and Reagan was out there with me. We had simply switched up. She was the shooting guard, playing on the left.

Which was a little weird because she was watching the game from the stands or above the stands or wherever she was when she visited me.

But it worked. It completely loosened me up. I made this great pass inside to Sandy. She grabbed it, turned, and tossed in a soft jumper before her defender knew what happened. The crowd cheered like crazy, and I gave the signal for full-court pressure. Mansfield struggled a bit, and when they got the ball to the other end, they hurried and Sandy intercepted a pass.

Soon, I raced toward the other end with the ball. I hesitated briefly before my no-look pass to Reagan, who was on the run to my left.

Prisha, actually playing on the left, was many steps behind the ball, which flew into a man's lap in the second row of the bleachers. She looked at me curiously as the man tossed it to the referee.

Reagan is not really on the floor, I reminded myself.

Mansfield scored to tie the game 51–51. We took the lead again when a Mansfield player plowed into Sandy and she made both free throws. Mansfield then tried a Starr-like bomb, which thudded against the front rim. It bounced straight at me. I grabbed it, turned, and started another fast break. I considered taking it all the way with a little juking, but I threw it outside to Reagan at the last minute.

The ball landed in the same man's lap.

Whoops.

"Sam, what are you doing?" yelled Coach Collins. "He's not on our team!" He shook his head as the man tossed the ball to the referee again. "Half court, half court!" Coach yelled.

I reminded myself that Reagan was not on this team. That she wasn't on this team because she had died. Starr was the starting point guard, and I was only filling in because Starr hurt her ankle. The days of Sam and Reagan were over. Pretending that Reagan was playing with me was not a good idea.

I focused on defense. I covered my man so well that she was out of the offensive picture. However, Mansfield scored when Jonesy got caught in a pick, freeing a Mansfield player to receive the ball in the paint and make an easy basket.

Tie game again.

Coach Collins called for a time-out.

I gulped water from the cup our manager handed me.

"You okay, Sam?" asked Coach Gray.

I nodded.

Sandy slapped my back. "Focus," she said. "Keep the ball on the court."

Coach Collins told us to maintain the pressure and play our game the final two minutes. I glanced at the stands. Dad gave me the thumbs-up. Luke and Brain D. looked a little concerned, but they cheered along with the crowd: "Go, Carlow Tigers, go!"

"Sam!" Sandy said. "Hands!"

I put my hands on top of all the others in the huddle.

"Play. Hard. Win!" we shouted.

Sandy threw a long pass to me, and I outran my defender for an easy layup.

We returned to a full-court press, but Mansfield dissected it easily and ran their inside-out play with authority. Prisha ran into a screen, and their wing guard launched a three-pointer that sailed through the net. Tie game again.

I brought the ball down the court, wondering why they weren't pressuring us. We ran play two, with no luck. I brought the ball back out and dribbled in place at the top. I signaled for the motion offense.

We executed that like pros. With a couple seconds left on the shot clock, Prisha caught her man off balance on her cut. I hit her for an easy layup.

The crowd exploded. The student section yelled, "Tiger in the tank, Tiger in the tank," and our mascot danced around the sideline. The referee shooed him back into his seat.

But Mansfield scored again on an outside shot. Tied again, 57–57.

Jonesy missed everything on a baseline jumper.

"Pressure!" screamed Sandy when the ref handed Mansfield the ball. And while they broke the press, we went crazy on defense. They threw up a prayer as their shot clock ran out. The ball barely hit the rim. Sandy grabbed the rebound. She threw it to me.

Ten seconds left in the game.

"Push it!" yelled Coach Collins. "Push it!"

And I did. I charged down the floor. I didn't hear the

crowd or feel my heart pound or care about the sweat dripping off my forehead. It was just me and the basketball.

And Reagan. When I spotted her ahead of her defender, I threw her a lead pass. To grab and put up her patent, game-winning shot.

She didn't catch it. The ball flew into the stands. The buzzer went off.

I couldn't believe Reagan missed my perfect pass. We had practiced the exact same play for years in the driveway. But things happen.

"Next time, Reagan!" I yelled.

In front of hundreds of people completely silent because their team had blown a great chance to beat rival Mansfield.

The timekeeper's mouth dropped open. His hand slipped on the buzzer and a half-baked *blip* sounded.

I had talked to Reagan in front of everybody. I couldn't pretend that it was the radio, or a phone call, or my practicing Spanish vocabulary words out loud. This was full-out crazy stuff in front of my whole world.

The Mansfield players ran past me to their bench, excited they had made it to overtime.

My teammates just stared at me. Finally, Sandy grabbed my arm and led me to the bench. "Are you for real?" she asked.

I knew to sit down.

Coach Collins looked at me like I was nuts.

"Maddie, take point!" Coach Collins yelled.

"For real?" asked Maddie.

"For real."

AFTERMATH

When the buzzer blew to end the game, which Mansfield won in overtime, it kept buzzing in my head. I heard it when I slapped hands with the Mansfield players in an autopilot way, although not so zombielike that I didn't hear a few of them say "Thanks for helping" under their breaths. And I heard it when I picked up my bag in the locker room, grabbed my jacket, and hurried out the back entrance. And I still heard it when I walked through the woods to a side street to avoid anything alive.

And the buzzer was still going off in my head when I walked down the road and Reagan yelled to hold up.

"Go away," I said.

That buzzer was like an electronic death knell without an off switch. And it was still on while I walked through the back entrance to Elliot Park.

A thin sheet of ice covered the duck pond. I sat on a bench and imagined the buzzing shifting to the tree speakers that played scratchy music when the ice was thick enough for skating. It would be a great start to a movie about the apocalypse.

Or maybe a movie about a personal apocalypse—the basketball career of Samantha Wilson crashes and burns.

I put my head in my hands and stared at the ice-crusted pond. I breathed in the freezing air. Gusts blew a battered snow-cone wrapper down the path. I shivered.

Finally, the buzzing in my head dimmed. And then it warbled and stopped.

Just like my basketball career.

I walked to the edge of the pond.

"Don't jump," said Reagan.

I shook my head.

"And don't trying walking on it. Even some of my more esteemed colleagues are unnerved by thin ice."

"What, water's okay but ice isn't?"

"Well, you know what Robert Frost said about ice."

"When did you start sitting in on my English class?"

"Someone needed to pay attention."

"Well, the pond's three feet deep, so you have nothing to worry about."

"I have plenty to worry about," said Reagan.

"Don't we all," I said.

"Speaking of which," said Reagan. "Maybe you should go back to the bench before you fall in."

I sat down again and hugged my jacket tight around me.

"You weren't on the floor, were you?" I said.

"No," said Reagan.

"You seemed so real."

"I know," said Reagan.

I shivered.

"But . . ."

"But what?" I asked.

"But I was imagining myself down there on the court with you," she said. "It was so hard to sit and watch—the only way I could cope was to pretend I was down there with you."

Nothing like a girl and her dead best friend both playing imaginary basketball.

I shook my head. "Please tell me you subbed in for someone and we didn't have six players on the court."

"I threw in some time travel so we played under the old-fashioned rules of six players on a side."

"Thank God."

The wind blew the snow cone wrapper back to the bench.

"But you really weren't on the court?" I asked.

"No."

"You looked real."

"Maybe you assumed I was there? You've passed to me a million times without looking."

"And you caught all of those passes."

Reagan laughed.

"No. I definitely saw you. In the flesh."

I shivered again.

"It's so cold," Reagan said.

I nodded.

I felt discombobulated. I stood. I picked up a stone and tried to skim it across the surface of the pond.

It broke through the icy crust right away and sank.

"I'm sorry if I screwed things up for you," Reagan said.

"Why? You weren't there."

I skimmed another stone. It skidded across the ice. It didn't sink.

"Okay, that's physically impossible," said Reagan.

I shook my head. "The theme of the night."

"Yeah, well."

I suddenly needed to be alone. Really alone. "I'll see you later, okay?"

"Sam!" she said.

"Later."

"Okay," she said.

I couldn't believe the cold. I zipped my jacket to the top and felt in my pockets for mittens that I knew weren't there. No hat, either. I put my gear bag strap on my shoulder, flipped up my collar, and shoved my hands into my pockets for the frozen walk home.

I barely hit the front steps before Mom flung open the door.

"Blue," she said. "Your lips are blue."

She yanked me into the house.

"Hot water," she told Dad, like I was about to birth a baby.

"Shower on," she told Luke, standing in the hall.

"Find some sweatpants and a sweatshirt," she told Bradley.

I don't know what was scarier—the fact that I started to shiver uncontrollably or Mom acting like a drill sergeant.

"I threw the ball into the stands once," said Bradley.

"Clothes," said Mom.

Luke laughed on his way up the stairs.

"Shower on!" Mom yelled.

She unzipped my jacket and took it off. She rubbed my arms like they were kindling and she was trying to start a fire.

I was so cold. I couldn't tell whether I was shivering or having seizures.

"God, Sam, what were you thinking? You went straight from being overheated in that warm gym to fifteen degrees." Mom frowned. "In your uniform. With bare legs. On the night we're setting new lows."

I shrugged, but it got lost in the shivers.

"You people have parkas!" she said. "Warm down parkas!"

Dad ran out of the kitchen with the electric water kettle.

"Tea, David, I wanted the water for tea."

"Right."

Dad turned and went back into the kitchen.

We both laughed, and then I started to cry.

"I'm sorry, Mom."

She held me.

"I'm sorry," said Mom.

"Tea, anyone?" said Dad, holding a coffee mug.

I couldn't help but laugh again.

Mom took the mug. "Here," she said. "We need to warm up your insides."

I reached for the mug, but my hands shook so much that I couldn't hold it.

Mom helped me guide it to my mouth, and I sipped it.

"Good," she said. "Now let's get you upstairs."

I stopped shivering somewhere between the ten- and fifteen-minute mark in the shower. Mom was sitting on the hall floor, back against the wall, when I came out of the bathroom wearing the ensemble that Bradley had selected—black sweats and navy hoodie, suspiciously the color scheme that appeared on my bed my first day of school.

But I wasn't in the mood for thinking.

I don't think I had ever seen Mom sit without her phone or a yellow pad or an appointment book. She walked me to my room, and I fell into bed.

The next morning, I woke up under my blanket, two comforters, and a quilt. I thought about staying there forever, but it got too warm and I figured I would have to face the music eventually.

"Want me to make you an instant breakfast?" asked Mom in the kitchen.

"I thought we were out," I said.

"I found your secret stash."

The eggshells and kid gloves were back in full force.

"Sure," I said.

She opened the door to the cellar. "David?" she called.

Oh, the instant breakfast would get us to the talking part faster.

I leaned back in my chair.

Mom made me a frothy drink with the blender—faster than stirring. She handed it to me as she and Dad sat down.

"How are you feeling?" asked Dad. "No pneumonia from last night?"

"Not yet," I said.

"Good," said Dad.

I sipped my breakfast.

"Do you want to tell us what happened at the game?" asked Mom.

I figured she didn't mean about the momentum shifting with a Carlow error and Mansfield regaining their shooting touch in overtime.

"I got confused," I said.

I went back to my drink.

"Confused how?" asked Dad.

"Okay, I thought I saw Reagan and I threw the ball to her," I said.

"Had she been there the whole game?" Mom asked.

"You mean on the left the whole game?" I asked.

"On the court, Sam," said Dad. "Anywhere on the court."

Whew. I hated lying to my parents. No need to tell them about Dead Reagan in the stands.

"No," I said. "She just showed up."

Literally and figuratively.

"And so you thought you saw her and you talked to her," said Mom.

"After she missed my pass," I said.

They both looked at me like I was crazy.

"Well, she missed it," I said. "It was an important pass."

Dad reached for Mom's hand. "And then what happened?"

"Then I realized I had tried to pass it to Reagan," I said. I hesitated. "But she's dead."

Mom closed her eyes. I didn't know whether she was trying to replay my performance in her head, or whether she was mortified at the validation of what she thought she had seen.

"And then she was gone?" asked Dad.

"Right."

Mom stirred her tea. Dad picked up my cup and put it into the sink. Then he sat down again.

"Has this happened before?" asked Mom.

"No," I said. "I didn't see Reagan on the court before that game."

No need to tell them that Dead Reagan had recently drummed up the courage to watch practices and games.

Dad narrowed his eyes. "Or anywhere else?"

"I haven't seen Reagan anywhere else," I said.

Like Dead Reagan had said, I couldn't see her.

"Sure?" asked Mom.

I nodded.

"Because well, sometimes we've heard you talking," he said.

"Well," said Mom, "mostly Bradley."

Bradley had credibility issues.

"So," Dad said, "we needed to ask."

I didn't say anything.

"Honey," Mom said, "this is probably very normal, you

know, imagining Reagan, after a traumatic ordeal."

Dad agreed. "And maybe we didn't handle things so well," he said. "We didn't get you the support you needed."

Mom took a long look at me. "It seemed like things were going better for you," she said. "And so we weren't that worried about your grades."

I nodded.

"You started to work out again," said Mom.

"You decided to try out for the team," Dad said.

"And you got right back on it after your suspension," added Mom.

"And you were making new friends," said Dad.

And then I threw a pass to a dead girl.

"Honey, you've resisted, but you don't have a choice now," Mom said. "You need to get some help. To help you deal with Reagan. With her death."

I tensed up. I knew this is where they were going, but I didn't want to talk to anybody. On the other hand, it was scary to have seen Reagan on the floor so clearly. It wasn't just some image like a hologram. It had been Reagan, three-dimensional real Reagan, and she was moving toward the baseline.

If she'd only caught the ball.

But what if she had caught the ball?

"Sam?" asked Mom.

"Yes?"

"So you will talk to someone?"

I needed to pay better attention to the reality thing.

"Yes," I said.

It might not be a bad idea. I couldn't convince myself that I hadn't seen Reagan moving toward that baseline.

"If we can work it in around practice."

Mom looked at Dad, and Dad looked at Mom.

Dad cleared his throat. "Honey, Coach Collins and I talked after the game on Friday. We agreed that you need to take a break."

"What?" I asked. "I'm kicked off the team? Again?"

"No, no," said Dad.

"So I'm suspended? For throwing the ball away? Like that's the first time that's happened in a high school basketball game?"

"Samantha," said Mom.

"I want to know!" I said.

"You need some time," Dad said. "To help you deal with things."

I shook my head. The truth was Coach Collins and my teammates probably didn't want me anywhere near the court. But now that I had started playing basketball again, I didn't know what else to do.

"I'll make some calls first thing Monday," said Mom. "We'll find the right person to help you." She reached for my shoulder. "Okay?"

I nodded.

BACK TO SCHOOL, II

Luke slowed down in front of school.

"I could drop you off and you could get it over with," he said.

"No thanks." I had prayed that all that walking around in the freezing-cold Friday night would produce the symptoms of a cold that would require home care, but I hadn't so much as sneezed during the weekend. And then I figured I might as well meet my fate.

But I didn't need to hurry.

"Sometimes ripping the Band-Aid off is the best thing."

I popped him.

"Ouch!"

He sped up and drove to his usual spot.

I kept seeing the packed gym on Friday night. In Mom's day, there would have been a couple dozen fans, max. But no, several hundred people had watched the ghost pass. By second period, the entire school would be talking about it.

Luke opened and shut his door and waited for me.

We headed to the gym entrance. I couldn't have walked more slowly. Luke put an arm around me, and he nodded at a couple kids who walked past us.

He opened the door. "Anyone gives you crap, you text me, okay?"

I nodded.

"I'm serious," he said. "I will take care of anyone who gives you a hard time."

"You sound like a Mafia guy."

"Call me Mob Man," he said.

"Haven't you cleaned enough uniforms?"

"The only team left is the winter track team and it's skimpy jerseys and shorts. I'll just throw their stuff into one of my regular washes," he said.

I laughed.

In Spanish, I thumbed through my dictionary. *Fantasma* was the word for "ghost," and *pelota* was the word for "ball." But wait, I looked up "basketball" and it was *baloncesto*. There were lots of words for "throw" and "toss." Halfway through class, I thought I had it right. *Pasé el baloncesto a un fantasma*. If anyone looked at me funny, I would shrug my shoulders like it was no big deal and say *Pasé el baloncesto a un fantasma*.

I drew some strange looks in the hall on the way to geometry. I got a smirk from an upper-class guy I didn't even know, and then he got shoved by someone behind me. I turned around to find Luke and Brain D. Luke nodded at Brain D. and Brain D. tugged at his ear like he had a listening device. It felt like I had a Secret Service detail. I didn't know whether to be mad or grateful.

The school newspaper sat on my desk, folded to the sports section. Brain D. grabbed it before I could read it.

"Show it," I said.

"Really, you don't need to see it," he said.

"It's online, too."

He put it back. The headline for our game was *Ghost Pass Fails Carlow Girls: Mansfield Wins in Overtime.*

Great.

"Hey," said Kevin.

Brain D. turned around and gave him a good stare.

"Not you—Sam," said Kevin.

Brain D. continued to stare.

Kevin ignored him.

"You doing okay?" asked Kevin.

I nodded.

"Sure?" he asked.

"Yup," I said. I tried to smile, but it's hard when you're so tense you can't move your lips. I would probably have lockjaw by the end of the day.

Mr. Pratt walked into the room when the bell struck class time.

He looked straight at me. And then he looked at Kevin, still leaning over to talk with me. His eyes narrowed.

"So, Ms. Wilson, how did that basketball game go?"

A couple kids in the back snickered.

He paused. "After you regained your academic eligibility?"

So much for student confidentiality.

The snickering stopped.

"Fine," I said.

"What an ass," Brain D. said under his breath.

"Well, I certainly hope you continue to make *passing* grades in my class," he said. He looked around the room, like he was expecting laughs for the punch line in a comedy routine.

I could feel the icy stares shot back at him. My classmates may have thought I was crazy, but I was still one of them and he wasn't.

Pratt turned to the whiteboard and began the day's lesson. You could tell he was mad by the way his face stayed red and how he clipped his speech, which made you think he was speaking more clearly, but I still couldn't understand anything he said about geometry. He left Kevin alone for the entire period.

I waited at the lunch line for Maddie and Jonesy, but after five minutes of not seeing them, I picked up a grilled cheese and found an empty table on the side of the cafeteria. It didn't take long to spot my former friends at a table of basketball players in the middle of the cafeteria. They were all laughing and joking and not looking for me.

I drank my milk slowly, feeling like the only kid kept inside for recess. I nibbled at the grilled cheese, but I wasn't hungry. I took one more bite for the sake of nutrition and headed to English class early. I sat with relief in the empty classroom, knowing that I would be spared looks and whispers for at least five minutes.

"Hey!" said Kevin. He took the seat beside me.

"Sudden interest in *A Separate Peace*?" I asked.

"Absolutely," he said.

"It doesn't end well," I said.

"Couldn't be worse than this," he said. He pulled out a ragged copy of *Romeo and Juliet*, its pages yellowed and the cover torn.

"I see you went for the antique model."

He laughed. "It's my mother's copy from college. She was an English major, and she wrote good notes on it."

I smiled.

"Sorry that Pratt was a prick in class," he said.

"Nothing unusual about that."

I meant that he had put up with it all year.

"It's not right," he said.

I shrugged.

"Well, I wanted to say that."

"Thanks," I said.

My English teacher, Mrs. Bates, walked into the room and looked surprised to see us. She nodded.

"I better go," said Kevin.

"Yeah."

He stuffed *Romeo and Juliet* into his backpack. He stood and took a few steps. Then he turned around. "You really okay?"

I nodded, and he walked away.

I was not okay.

But I made it through the afternoon. I almost texted Luke when some idiot everyone called Not-Sheldon pretended to chest pass to his geek friend in the hall. But it was hard to take the insult seriously when I knew that not only could his friend not catch a real pass, but a single one of mine could knock them both over. So I smiled and kept on walking. Kids like that were why God created dodgeball.

I threw all my books into my locker. I wasn't in the mood for homework. What was the point?

Outside, I spotted Mom waiting in her car.

I opened the passenger door.

"Hi, sweetie," she said. "Nothing's wrong."

"Okay." I got in and fastened the seat belt. "So . . ."

"Can't a mother pick up her kid from school?" she asked.

"Maybe when the kid is five," I said.

"All right," she said. "I got you an appointment with a psychologist. A good one, I am told. Today at three thirty."

I didn't say anything.

"It's time," she said. "It's past time."

I sighed. "I know."

She squeezed my shoulder. And then she started the car.

Over the river and through the woods, off to the shrink I go.

FOOTPRINTS

Reagan showed up after Kevin walked me home from school on Tuesday. I sat on the front steps. It was cold, and it was already getting dark.

"So how was talking to the psychologist?" she asked.

"Better than I thought," I said.

I stared at the Christmas lights strung along the opposite porch.

"Besides, you probably heard the whole thing."

"No," Reagan said. "That's confidential."

I shook my head. I would never understand the rules for the Dead Dribble Queen. "I keep thinking you see everything."

"No," said Reagan. "That's not me."

The lights to a manger scene in front of the porch came on in case I didn't get it.

"Did you tell her about us?" Reagan asked.

"No," I said. "Well, I had to tell her about seeing you on

the court. Or thinking I saw you on the court—there's a difference, you know."

Reagan laughed. "I can see your mom filling out the form now: Depressed? Yes. Anxious? Yes. Passing to dead friends? Yes."

"Very funny," I said. "Almost as funny as making the student newspaper."

Reagan laughed. "Was I in the box score?"

"Zero points for Reagan Murphy."

"Now that's not funny!" she said. "See, if I was really there, I would have scored."

"You're obnoxious," I said.

I flicked a snow flurry off my jacket. "But I didn't tell her about us—the now us. That's between you and me."

"I'm glad you're seeing her," Reagan said. "That pass freaked me out."

"I have to ask again," I said.

"Okay."

"You weren't there, right? I mean, on the court?"

"No," said Reagan.

"Just checking." I frowned. "So, I was seeing things."

"Afraid so. I was as surprised as everybody else."

I nodded. Although there's something strange about your dead friend telling you about your pass to the delusional form of herself.

"It's too cold to sit," I said. "Let's walk."

"Okay."

The flurries increased as we strolled past more holiday

lights. I wondered if Reagan's parents had put theirs up yet. Reagan was a master at straightening out Christmas lights, and she would set them out in her backyard and patiently untangle every strand. I sat at her picnic table a few times, holding a cup of hot chocolate in my mittened hands, and we talked while she untangled.

Maybe Reagan's parents would skip Christmas this year, with no one to do the untangling. And no kid to open their presents.

"You're spacing out on me," Reagan said.

I shook my head. "Just thinking."

"Why do you think you saw me on the court?"

"I don't know," I said. "I heard you in the stands a few times, but I couldn't hear you at the end."

"I was screaming my head off," Reagan said.

"But so was everyone else."

"I hate losing to Mansfield."

I shrugged. "I lost my confidence. So I pretended you were on the court with me."

"So you started out pretending," she said. "Like me."

"Right."

"Go on."

"I couldn't do it without you," I said.

"But you were playing fine," Reagan said.

"It didn't feel that way," I said.

"And you live for game situations like that."

"I lived for game situations like that with you."

Reagan didn't respond.

A couple of kids ran past us, trying to knock each other into the snow collecting on the ground.

"And then I pushed the ball up the court and you were right on the wing like you were supposed to be. So I passed you the ball."

"And delusional me missed it."

"Totally. Like a little kid who forgets you can pass without looking."

"Sorry I missed the ball."

"Don't apologize for your delusional self," I said. "It's not your fault."

"You play a great point," Reagan said. "You always did. Coaches played me there because you're a better shooting guard."

"Not true," I said.

"Well, there is my spectacular dribbling."

"Right."

"Who knew the Dribble Queen competition would launch my point guard career?"

"Confidence was never an issue for you, was it?"

Reagan laughed.

"Not funny."

"Look, for the record, I wasn't always there," she said.

"What do you mean?"

"Remember when I broke my wrist? When we were ten?"

I didn't. I stopped walking at the entrance to Elliot Park. The snow was coming down seriously now, filling in the steps of a runner who had turned from the sidewalk into the park path.

"I broke it skating here," she said.

I remembered. "For some bizarre reason you tried to do a double axel."

"We'd just watched figure skating on tv. It looked easy."

"You fell hard," I said, wincing with the memory.

"It really hurt."

We'd tried to keep skating, but Reagan was in too much pain. So we walked home and Mom carted her off to the ER.

"And you insisted on coming to practice with your cast. You tried to convince Coach Angela that you could play one-handed."

"I could have," she said. "But my point is that you've played basketball plenty of times without me and played great."

I nodded. I had scored twenty points in the league championship game a couple weeks later. I was named MVP.

"Whenever I looked at the bench, you were sitting with your arms crossed, pink cast on top, pouting!"

"M before W," said Reagan.

"Right side up or upside down," I said.

"It's going to be okay," Reagan said.

"But everyone thinks I'm crazy," I said. "It's like I'm a modern-day witch."

"I think you're exaggerating."

"And *The Scarlet Letter* is coming up next in English. Perfect timing."

"At least I won't have to read that," Reagan said.

I laughed. I couldn't help it.

"Everyone doesn't think you're crazy," said Reagan. "I don't."

"Thanks," I said.

"Later," said Reagan.

"See you," I said.

And I just stood there, watching the footprints fill up with snow, until they were completely erased.

BLACK THURSDAY

I knew Mr. Pratt would get his retribution for having to grade me on demand. But he didn't go after me—he went after Kevin. He must have figured out Kevin was a friend, and he couldn't go after the depressed girl so he went after him. He called on Kevin to discuss a homework problem first thing that week, knowing that he would refuse. And then he called on him over and over in class on Tuesday, and he added detention after detention when Kevin refused to answer his questions.

Kevin came to class. He wrote down answers for quizzes. So he didn't turn in all his homework and he didn't have the Auto-Raise button installed on his arm. Who cared? Kevin was the one person who treated me exactly the same after the ghost pass, except for checking in because he was worried about me.

And then it rained on Wednesday. And Kevin was late for school by a whole class and he hurried into geometry wearing a long black trench coat with water dripping off it. Along with his black pants, black T-shirt, and new black boots.

But Mr. Pratt saw an opportunity when he stopped mumbling to his own shoes and looked up. He actually smirked. "You, me, principal's office, now!"

Kevin rolled his eyes. But he stood and followed Mr. Pratt, leaving his backpack under his chair.

"Don't just leave that here!" Mr. Pratt said.

When Pratt looked away, Kevin slipped me his sketchbook and then he put his backpack over his shoulder and followed Mr. Pratt down the hall. His new boots clunked all the way. Mr. Pratt returned, but Kevin did not.

"What the heck?" I said to myself.

"Trench coat," said Brain D.

"What?"

"Strictly prohibited," he said.

"You're kidding. Kevin wore his raincoat into class because he was late!"

Brain D. shook his head. "Double button front closure. Trench coat."

"Unbelievable."

I found Kevin at his locker on the way to lunch. I handed back his notebook.

"Thanks," he said. "I didn't want it confiscated or whatever."

"Trench coat?" I asked.

He nodded. "Pratt finally got me." He shook his head. "Principal Carson said wearing a trench coat is a major dress-code violation so he didn't have any choice."

"Seriously?"

"It could hide weapons."

"Any other teacher would have told you to shove it in your locker."

"I know."

"Are you suspended?" I asked.

"In-school suspension."

"First amendment?" I asked. "We have rights."

"School," said Kevin. "No amendments, no rights."

"I keep forgetting."

He shrugged. "You know what's funny? Mom told me to take my dad's raincoat because it was pouring. I never wear them. Who does? But for once, I did what she said."

"Are you stuck in detention all day?" I asked.

"Not if I get a parent to come in for a discussion."

"Are they coming?"

He shook his head. "Dad's away on business, and my mom is a nurse on a day shift. I'll deal with study hall."

"Did they call the bomb squad to blow up your backpack?"

Kevin laughed. "Principal Carson asked if he could look through it. He rummaged around and came up with a bunch of geometry assignments and handed them to Mr. Pratt."

"Unbelievable," I said.

I thought about Kevin all afternoon. No way that Mr. Pratt and the school board could get away with this crap. But I didn't know what to do about it. I looked into the ninth-grade study hall on the way out of school, but it was empty. Maybe they had a secret study room for students with in-school suspension.

The rain had mostly stopped, so I walked home, hoping

that Reagan would join me. Maybe she'd know what to do. I had no idea how you dealt with a school board and its absurd rules. And Pratt had been gunning for Kevin the entire year. Speaking of weapons. Kevin deserved better, especially when he was being so nice to me.

But Reagan didn't show up. It was drizzling, but that really shouldn't matter to someone who didn't have to worry about catching colds.

I talked about Kevin at supper.

"So Boy in Black gets in trouble because he wore black clothes?" asked Bradley.

"Pretty much," I said.

"What else is a Boy in Black supposed to wear?"

We laughed.

"Good point, son," said Dad.

"Mrs. Turner told Eloise that a rubber band wasn't a bracelet last year, and me and Tim wore rubber bands the rest of the week."

"Did Mrs. Turner tell you guys that rubber bands weren't bracelets?" I asked.

"No," said Bradley. "She only picked on Eloise."

Eloise was a neighborhood girl who had some development issues. Bradley could be oblivious to many things, but he and his buddies were on high alert for any slight of Eloise.

I sat straight up. "That's it, Bradley."

"Rubber bands? I got a bunch left if you need them."

"No," I said. "Black. My geometry class should wear black!"

"That would sure piss off Pratt!" said Luke.

"Language, Luke," said Mom.

"That would surely irritate Mr. Pratt," said Luke.

Mom glared at him. "Is the laundry done?" she asked.

"Washed, dried, and folded," he said.

"Good."

I had a black skirt. And a black blazer. And a black Nike workout T-shirt. And my trusty black Sperrys. But would anybody go along with me besides Brain D.? I wasn't exactly Miss Popularity, and that's before I threw the ball to my dead teammate. I could spread the idea with #notpratt, but I really needed someone like Brain D. to get involved.

"Hey, Luke, can you see if Brain D. would do it?"

"Even better, I'll call Christie, his girlfriend."

"Sam," said Mom, "is this really a good idea? I mean, well, you've just had a bad experience." She hesitated. "And, you know . . ."

"There's nothing illegal about the color black," I said. "In fact, I've had to wear it more than I planned this year."

Mom reached over and grabbed my hand. "I know, honey. I wonder if now is a good time to get involved in any, you know, dissension."

When I just started talking to a psychologist about playing basketball with dead people.

"I'm not throwing school property in the fountain," I said, looking at Luke. "I'm coordinating classroom fashion."

"I think it's a great idea," said Dad.

"Don't encourage her," said Mom.

Dad winked. Luke high-fived me over the pot roast platter.

"Do it, sis," he said.

I decided to make it happen. Luke wasn't the only family member who could support Kevin. And besides, if Mr. Pratt was annoyed with Coach Gray, he should have dealt with me, not Kevin. I thought about my own outfit. I could throw in some black tights. No, I could do better. I could dye my hair black. That would be a statement.

Yes!

"Luke, can you take me to the drugstore?" I asked. "I need some supplies."

"What, honey?" asked Mom.

"Oh, this and that. Some stupid biology project."

Luke wiped his mouth with his napkin. "Let's go," he said. "I need gas, anyway."

The next morning, I stood in front of my mirror and admired myself. I looked even better in my new black hair than I did when I dressed as Morticia from *The Addams Family* at Halloween a few years ago. I might have overdone the pink highlights, but I thought they were a perfect accent. And the black drop earrings that Luke had found in the costume jewelry section were superb. What was it with him and his taste in jewelry? I pulled back my blazer sleeve to uncover a tattoo of a black spider. Luke had found these great fake tattoos in the toy section. He bought himself one of an exploding eight ball.

I walked into the kitchen. Mom turned from the sink.

She screamed.

A really loud, bloodcurdling scream.

Bradley ran down the stairs in his undershirt and unzipped school pants. "Mouse in the house!" he yelled. "Mouse in the house!"

Dad ran down the stairs, too. "Donna?"

Mom pointed at me.

Dad stared. His eyebrows raised.

"Ah, nothing's pierced, I hope," he said.

"No, but I got this." I exposed the spider.

Mom's eyes popped. "Please tell me it's not real!"

"Cool," said Bradley.

Luke stumbled down the stairs. "God, you people," he said, still rubbing sleep out of his eyes even though he was dressed for school.

"Just take a look at what your sister's done," said Mom. She lifted a strand of my jet-black hair. And she showed him the spider.

He pulled up his sleeve to expose his exploding eight ball.

"Have you both lost your minds?" Mom yelled.

"Cool!" said Bradley. "Do you have any more?"

"Son?" asked Dad.

"Chill," Luke said. "They're fake."

Mom looked at me. "The dye washes out, right?"

I shrugged. "I think so. But the packages in the drugstore all looked alike, and I was in a hurry."

Dad grinned.

Mom sank into her chair.

Luke and I laughed like hyenas all the way to school.

I was nervous walking down the hall to Spanish. I did get

a few "definitely" responses from my email and tweet last night. And I knew Brain D. was in action, but I was the girl of passing ill repute a few days ago. But, if a few kids besides Brain D. and I dressed in black for Kevin, it would make a statement. My hair got a few stares in Spanish, and there might have been one more black T-shirt than usual, but that was it.

I ducked into the bathroom between classes. I needed to take the pink down a notch.

I was unprepared for the sea of black that met me in geometry.

"Hurry," said Brain D. He pointed at the clock.

Several kids gave me the thumbs-up as I slipped into my seat.

The bell rang. Mr. Pratt walked into the room. His mouth dropped open when he saw us.

"What the . . ."

I don't know if it was Cornell Schaeffer's vintage Black Panther T-shirt from his grandfather, or my pink highlights, or Brain D.'s "Black Is the New Black" T-shirt, or Diggers swimming in his father's black suit. Or maybe it was Eileen Thompson wearing her sister's black waitress outfit, complete with black velvet ribbon in her hair.

Mr. Pratt closed his mouth. He shook his head.

Kevin shuffled in late, wearing tan khakis and yellow golf shirt. His hair was still wet from his shower, and it was streak-free. He gave me a sad smile.

He didn't realize what was going on until he started to sit down.

His eyes widened as he looked around the room.

"Oh my God," Kevin said. A huge grin erupted on his face.

He sat with authority.

"Here, dude," said Brain D. "We made some at the mall last night." He handed Kevin a "Black Is the New Black" T-shirt.

Kevin whipped off his polo shirt and replaced it with the T-shirt. In full view of Mr. Pratt, who looked as white as, well, a ghost. One subversive kid was an opportunity, but twenty of us was a threat.

Kevin folded his arms and stared straight at Mr. Pratt. "Any questions today, sir?" he asked.

Mr. Pratt's face grew red. He pursed his lips together so hard that they turned white. His eyes narrowed. He stared back at Kevin.

Then he shook his head. That might have been for Kevin. Then he shook his head again. I think that was for kids in general, but I took it personally.

Mr. Pratt turned to the whiteboard and began the day's lesson.

Someone began clapping. Soon, we were all clapping.

Mr. Pratt turned around, mystified.

Then we stopped clapping. And Mr. Pratt, his face redder, turned back to the board. Evidently wearing black didn't qualify as a reportable offense.

Brain D. high-fived Kevin, and so did a few other boys. And Kevin gave me the sweetest smile in the world.

"Good stuff, Sam," whispered Brain D.

I was pretty sure that the dye I bought was the kind that you can rinse out when you want. But if not, well, maybe black was the new black.

Mr. Pratt didn't call on Kevin the entire class.

But Kevin kept grinning at me, and I kept grinning back at him.

Sam-I-am. Making things happen.

BACK IN BLACK

The story of Black Thursday got around school, and on Friday, lots of kids wore black, including Luke's entire basketball team. Except for Drew Carson. I wore more than I intended, as it turns out even temporary black hair dye lasts a few weeks. Bradley wore his black *Star Wars* shirt, and Mom even let him apply the extra spider tattoo to his forearm as long as he promised to keep his sleeves down inside school.

When I hit the lunch line, I found Starr Regal standing next to the milk cartons with her crutches, like she was waiting for someone.

"I like your hair," she told me.

"Thanks," I said.

"Sit with me?" she asked.

I didn't know what to say.

"It means you'll have to put my stuff on your tray," she said, pointing to the crutches.

"No problem."

I went through the line with Starr crutch-stepping beside me. I offered her the same chicken wrap and salad that I picked out. Then I carried our identical lunches to an empty table at the back of the cafeteria.

"How much longer?" I asked when she leaned the crutches against the wall.

"I'm not sure," she said. "I see the doctor again after school. I'm thinking another week of crutches and then PT."

"Sounds like you know the drill," I said.

She nodded. "I wish I could trade my ankle for a new one."

I started in on my food, wondering why Twinks wasn't eating at the players' table.

"Look, I know I'm new and everything, but we have a good team," she said.

I shrugged. Carlow High was known for its basketball. Last year's mediocre season was unusual.

"A lot better than I thought," she said.

I got it. Big star from California set a low expectation bar for little New Hampshire.

She read my face like a book. "That's not what I meant," she said.

"Right."

"Okay, I didn't want to come here," she said. "But my mom's job got moved, and so I didn't have a choice."

She bit into her wrap. And frowned. "Sorry. Any wrap is better in California."

"Just put some maple syrup on it," I said.

She burst out laughing.

"Anyway, I can't play yet, but you can." She hesitated. "How do we get you back?"

I motioned toward the players' table. "We?"

She shrugged. "They're a little freaked out," she said. "Maddie and Jonesy told us you're different now, and then, well, you know, passing the ball like that . . ."

"And you're not freaked out?"

"I'm from California. If you're not seeing things, you have a psychic who does."

I smiled. I drank some milk.

"So?" she said. "Will you come back? As long as I have to sit, I'd like to watch good basketball."

"You know I'm unofficially suspended, right?"

"I thought you quit," said Starr. "Coach Collins doesn't do details."

I shook my head.

"So? How long are you unofficially suspended?"

"I don't know," I said.

"Then talk with Coach Collins," she said. "Please. I don't know how much longer I can take Maddie and Jonesy running into each other."

I smiled.

Dad dropped Bradley and me off at our game that night. We took seats at the top of the bleachers, half full since Luke's team was playing an away game at Bishop Hardy.

Sure enough, Maddie and Jonesy ran into each other within seconds of the opening jump ball.

Bradley giggled. "I thought only my team does that."

"Very funny," I said.

We settled down after handing Twin Mountain Regional a six-point lead, and the teams traded baskets for several minutes without the help of turnovers or fouls.

"That's better," said Reagan.

I nodded.

We traded missed shots for a couple of minutes.

"Boring," said Bradley. "I'm getting popcorn."

"Okay," I said.

He held out his palm.

"Dad gave you money," I said.

"Not popcorn money."

I handed him a five. "Take your time," I said. "Get me some, too."

"He's so cute," said Reagan.

"Right," I said.

"My little Bradley is growing up."

"Into a con artist," I said.

On the court, Maddie stood at the top of the key, dribbling, while she watched her teammates put the current play into action. Jonesy posted up at the foul line, Sandy and Maya crossed underneath, and Prisha swung wide. Maddie hit Jonesy with the pass and she whipped it to Prisha, who put it through the basket for two points.

"Nice," I said.

"Not bad," said Reagan. "But we need you out there."

"Funny, that's what Starr told me."

"The Twinkster is right," said Reagan. "What are you going to do about it?"

I shifted on the hard bleacher. "Maybe talk with Coach Collins next week."

"I meant a definite plan."

I thought. "Okay, the real plan is that I talk with Mom and Dad this weekend. They'll tell me to talk to Dr. Philips about it. I will. Maybe even Monday. And then, first thing Tuesday morning, I'll talk to Coach Collins."

"Better."

We watched the rest of the first period. The teams broke for their benches with the game tied.

"I'm afraid it might happen again," I said.

"Seeing me on the court?" said Reagan.

"Yes."

"We could practice now," she said. "I'm here, not down there. I'm here, not down there."

"Very funny."

"Everybody sing with me," Reagan said. "I'm here, not down there. I'm here, not down there," she said again in a sing-song voice.

"Stop now, please," I said.

"Sorry. We can only sing hymns upstairs."

I shook my head. I watched play resume on the court. As hard as it was to watch my team from the bench, it was even harder to watch from the stands. I had to get back on the floor. And I had to stay there.

"Reagan?"

"Yes?"

"I hate to say it, but maybe it would be better if you didn't come to my games," I said.

"You want me here, you don't want me here . . ."

"I know," I said. "I'm sorry."

I felt like crying. I wanted Reagan there more than anything else in the world. But I couldn't keep seeing her on the court, too, and I didn't know how to turn that off. I didn't expect a therapist's office to be magic.

"Hey, it's okay," she said. "You can tell me about the games later."

I nodded.

"Hey!" yelled Bradley. Kevin followed him up the bleachers. "Look who I found!"

Kevin waved as they climbed two more rows to our seats.

"Boy in Black has blue jeans!" said Bradley.

Kevin rolled his eyes.

"Enough, Bradley," I said.

"Mind if I sit with you?" asked Kevin.

"Please," I said.

He looked at the scoreboard. "Looks like we're hanging in without you and Starr."

"It would be a rout if you were on the floor," Reagan whispered.

I smiled.

"I'll see you out there soon, right?" Kevin said.

"You bet," said Reagan.

I smiled broadly.

Kevin looked at me curiously, like he knew my reactions weren't exactly matching his comments.

"See ya," said Reagan.

"Did you bring me some popcorn?" I asked Bradley.

"Was I supposed to?"

"That was the get-me-some-too part."

He sighed. "Okay." He scampered down the bleachers.

"That gives us five minutes of peace," I told Kevin. "And more if there's a single distraction in the hall."

"I like Bradley," Kevin said.

"He wore his black *Star Wars* shirt to school today."

"Cool." Kevin smiled.

And Kevin and I, and eventually Bradley, watched the rest of the game. We played hard, and Maddie and Jonesy stopped running into each other, but we were outmatched. We lost by twelve points.

I sat in the living room armchair Monday night, waiting for Mom and Dad. Plan A had become plan B over the weekend, as they turned it into their annual holiday shopping spree, and they were hardly home. So I had started with Dr. Philips. Black Thursday got major points on the back-in-action scale. She liked my pink highlights, too. She was okay with my playing again as long as I kept seeing her. And not Reagan.

I took a deep breath when Mom came into the room holding her favorite teacup and Dad walked in behind her. They sat on the couch.

"You wanted to talk to us?" asked Mom.

"Yes," I said. I took another deep breath. "I want to ask Coach Collins about coming back."

"So soon?" asked Dad.

"Oh, I don't know, honey," said Mom.

"Dr. Philips said it would be okay," I said.

"We don't want to make another mistake," said Mom.

Dad nodded.

"We should have made you see a therapist months ago," Mom said.

I didn't know how to answer. I sat back in the armchair. This was going to be harder than I thought.

"We should have been talking with your teachers about your schoolwork," said Mom.

"We should have listened to Bradley when he told us you were talking to someone in your room," Dad said.

"Maybe we shouldn't have pushed you to play ball again so soon," Mom said.

They shook their heads at what lousy parents they had been.

Luke stuck his head in the doorway. "Okay if I head out for a while?"

"No!" Mom replied.

"Really?" said Luke.

"Help Bradley with his homework," said Dad.

"O-kay," said Luke, shaking his head. He gave me the look that said, "What grief have you brought down upon us now?"

I shrugged.

"Now, Samantha," said Mom, "it hasn't been that long. Since . . ."

"Since the ghost pass," I said. "That's what they call it in school."

Mom closed her eyes.

"We don't want you to go back too early," said Dad.

"This is already the second time you've been suspended from the team," Mom said.

"Practice makes perfect," I said.

No return laughter. I had to work on my act.

"And you're sure that Dr. Philips said it was okay," said Dad. "It seems so early."

"You can call her if you want," I said.

"We believe you," said Mom.

"And you don't think, well, you don't think you'll have the same issue again?" asked Dad. "I mean, on the court?"

"I'm not going to pass to Reagan again," I said.

Dad grimaced.

"Oh, honey, how can you be so sure?" asked Mom.

I couldn't very well tell her that Dead Reagan and I had an arrangement.

"We want to be careful," said Dad. "We need to take better care of you."

"And you did and I am talking to a psychologist. And it's okay with her, and it's fine with me if you ask her."

"Your sessions are between you and Dr. Philips," Mom said.

"Well, she really liked Black Thursday," I said.

Dad beamed. "I am so proud of you for that."

Mom looked at my hair and sighed.

I figured it wasn't the time to tell her I was thinking of keeping it black for the entire basketball season.

"So can I talk with Coach Collins tomorrow or not?" I said. "I have a lot of homework to do."

Mom looked at Dad and Dad looked at Mom and then they both looked at me.

"If this is what you really want," Mom said.

"And if you promise to tell us the minute school gets too hard or basketball gets too hard or anything else gets too hard," said Dad.

I smiled. "I thought life was supposed to be hard."

"It shouldn't be this hard for a kid," said Dad. He did not smile.

"And Reagan shouldn't have gotten a bum heart," I said.

"No," said Dad softly.

Mom looked like she was ready to cry.

"I promise I will tell you if things go south."

Mom didn't look much better with that.

"Okay, here's the deal," I said. "I promise I will check in with you every day and tell you honestly how things are going." I hesitated. "I swear."

"That would help," said Mom.

"Go do your homework," said Dad. "And good luck talking with Coach Collins."

"Thanks," I said.

I ran up the stairs. Both Luke and Bradley were singing the Marines' Hymn as loud as they could in Bradley's bedroom. Great. Nothing like a Greek chorus for Spanish vocabulary.

Dad drove me to school early the next morning. I knocked on Coach Collins's closed door, but I didn't hear anything. I leaned against the corridor wall and waited. Eventually, he walked down the hallway in sweatpants and running shoes. He took off his black wool cap.

"How long have you been waiting?" he asked.

"Ten minutes max. I wanted to make sure I caught you."

He opened his office door. He unzipped his jacket and sat behind his desk. I sank into the metal folding chair reserved for guests.

"What can I do for you?" he asked.

"Well," I said. "I want to come back on the team."

He stared at me. "It hasn't been your year, has it?"

I shrugged.

"Is your schoolwork still going better?" he asked.

I nodded.

"And otherwise?" he asked. "I heard you were part of a disruption in geometry class."

"We just wore black clothes," I said.

"Well, I heard that Mr. Pratt saw red!" He chuckled. "Coach Gray seemed tickled about it." He paused. "No disciplinary actions? Detentions or anything?"

I shook my head. "We just wore black."

He smiled. Then he looked serious. "I need to know from

you that you're okay," he said. "Your father called me last night, and we talked, but I need you to tell me that you're okay."

"I'm okay," I said.

"Well, same deal as last time. No promises about starting, and you've got a lot of running to make up."

I was back on the team! I grinned.

"Keep the ball on the court, okay?"

"Okay."

I got up.

"Thanks, Coach," I said. "And I'm ready to go." I picked up my gear bag and raised it high.

"See you at practice," he said.

I ran down the hall, grinning like a fool. But when I passed the gym door, I stopped. I opened it. Dim light floated through the small high windows on the far wall. I walked to the center of the court. I closed my eyes and took a deep breath.

I am back, I thought. Really back.

RIP

A week later, we took the bus to Newtonville. I sat in the back row, watching the trees roll by, some of them with leftover snow on their lowest branches. I had talked with Dr. Philips four times now, and it wasn't the worst thing that ever happened to me. No way I would tell her about me and Dead Reagan, but I liked spending time with her. It was nice talking to someone who wasn't related and didn't know me from the sports pages. Although it's beyond me how someone could grow up in America and not know about the full-court press.

The bus bounced over a frost heave.

Sandy got up and walked toward me.

"Okay if I sit here?" she asked, pointing to the empty space beside me.

I wondered if she thought I left a space for Reagan.

I looked up at her. She smiled. Like normal.

"Sure," I said.

"Coach Collins talked to us," she said. "To the seniors."

I nodded.

"I know Reagan was never actually on this team, but she would have made it."

Dribble Queens always do.

"And so we thought we should honor her, you know, show how much we miss her."

I didn't understand.

"We'd like to dedicate today's game to Reagan."

I didn't know what to say.

"If it's okay with you," she said. "We want to have a silent moment in the huddle, and then we'll dedicate the game to Reagan."

That would be nice, I thought. "Okay."

She hesitated. "It was Starr's idea. And I'm pretty embarrassed that we didn't think of it earlier since some of us knew Reagan."

"It's okay," I said.

Twinks was turning out fine.

"You don't have to say anything," Sandy said. "We wanted to do it."

And so exactly that happened before the tip-off. Coach Collins said that the team had a hole without Reagan, and not because we had lost the first two games.

"Let's bow our heads, and think about Reagan, and remember how hard this year is for Sam, her best friend," said Sandy.

Heads went down, and Sandy put her arm around me.

I love you, Reagan, I whispered.

"Okay, hands in the middle," said Sandy. "This one's for Reagan Murphy!"

"Reagan, Reagan, Reagan," we yelled.

Sandy showed me the bottom of her shoe. Written in black marker was *RIP RM*. Other players showed me the same writing on their shoes. Starr pointed to a black ribbon wrapped around the handle of her crutch.

That was so cool.

Maddie reached over and we fist-bumped.

I felt bad that I kept Dead Reagan away from her own dedication.

"Okay, back together," said Sandy.

We put our hands together in the middle of our huddle.

"Play. Hard. Win."

Coach Collins started me at point guard. Maddie had refused to play there ever again.

We lost the tip-off, and Newtonville hurried up the court, but Sandy got in the way of a first shot and slammed it toward me. I picked it up after one bounce and started the transition. Prisha hustled up the left side, and Maya moved up the right. I put a lead pass in front of Prisha, but it bounced right into the bleachers.

Here we go again.

Then Prisha yelled, "Sorry, I had it, but then I slipped."

The referee supervised a Newtonville throw-in.

"Next time," said Prisha and pointed at me.

I could feel my entire team breathe a sigh of relief.

I reached down and touched the spot on the bottom of my

basketball shoe where I had drawn two half hearts with a Magic Marker. I touched it after each of my field goals, and I touched it again when the buzzer went off and we won.

LONG VIEW

The next morning, I was still excited from winning the game. I woke up way too early, but there was no way I could go back to sleep. I threw open the drapes to find the first serious snowfall of the season—at least three inches.

I wanted to be in it.

I dressed in layers and found my ski gloves. Then I hurried to the garage and pulled out my mountain bike. If Kevin could play golf in the snow, I could ride my bicycle in it. I half pedaled and half slid my bike down the driveway. It was freezing, and I pulled my wool cap over my ears. I zipped my parka all the way up and headed into the street.

I had a blast making tire tracks on the untouched snow on the side of the road. A few drivers gave me strange looks, but I didn't care. It was slippery, and I wished I'd thought to tie something on the bike carrier for traction, like the bags of sand Dad kept in the car trunks. I laughed, thinking about a pail of sand from the backyard sandbox perched behind me.

I rode with my breath freezing in the air and the tires blazing a new path past the stores on Main Street. It was slow going but exhilarating. I stopped to catch my breath at the huge oak tree at the intersection of Long Road and Dairy Road, home of the North Congregational Church. A single leaf dangled from the farthest reaches of the lowest, snow-covered limb. An old basketball hoop with metal chains was nailed to a backboard at one end of the church parking lot.

I steadied myself with one hand on the tree, and I tapped snow off the bike chain and the derailleur. Then I looked at the snow-draped trees hovering over Long Road. The road looked even more magical in winter than in the summer, when Reagan and I took long rides past luscious green leaves, or the fall, when we rode past bright red apples in the orchard. The road was usually empty, and it felt like our secret kingdom. Reagan and I made it a different place each time, like Neverland, Narnia, or Fantasyland.

"Nice game last night," said Reagan.

"How do you know?" I asked.

"I can read a morning newspaper," she said.

"Oh. Right."

"So tell me," she said.

"It felt great," I said.

"Awesome."

The wind picked up and knocked snow from tree branches.

"Come on," said Reagan.

"What?"

"Let's ride down Long Road again."

"You don't have your bike," I said.

"Sam."

"What?"

"I keep telling you I don't have superpowers. I couldn't pedal a bike in my present condition."

"So?"

"We'll double ride."

"Oh no."

The last time we rode double, Reagan launched us into a ditch. She escaped with scrapes and bruises, but I sprained the heck out of my ankle and missed a week of basketball camp.

"Why not?"

"The ditch? Remember?"

Reagan giggled. "Oh, yeah. Well, remember I'm already dead, so that's not an issue for me."

"Well, I'm not," I said.

"I know."

I sighed. "Okay."

I picked up my bike and rolled it to the road. I hopped on and pedaled.

"Scoot up," said Reagan.

"You've got to be kidding."

"I am not."

I scooted up so invisible Dead Reagan could have more room.

The cold wind was invigorating. I gripped the handlebar harder when my bike slid on unseen ice. The mountain bike treads that are great for mud don't do a thing for ice.

We started down Long Road. A gust blew snow off the trees along the road and dusted us.

"Sweet!" yelled Reagan. "I can't believe we didn't come out here in the winter before!"

"It's beautiful," I said.

I hit another skid.

"Hey, be careful," said Reagan. "Just because I'm already dead doesn't mean I want to fall."

"Right," I said, but not understanding. "Hey, where are we this time? The Land of the Giants? The outer galaxy?" I paused. "Heaven?"

"Not funny."

I concentrated on pedaling steady, which was tough on unpacked snow. I had this vision of Reagan standing in snow-like clouds.

"And you get to be the teen angel."

"It's teen-angel nation," she said. "There's so many of us there's a rotation. Like the milk monitor in elementary school."

"Please don't say there's no crying over spilled milk."

"And there's no running with scissors."

We laughed hysterically.

I swerved again.

"Geez! You need to practice your snow steering," said Reagan.

"Yeah, yeah. Practice. It's everything."

I slowed down.

"So, location. Where are we?" I asked.

"The snowy mountains of Austria."

"And we're picking up stray von Trapps as they hike over the hills to escape the Nazis."

"I don't think it was in the winter, though," said Reagan. "At least not in the movie."

"The movie never does the real story justice."

"True."

I imagined the road was a trail winding past wind-blasted boulders.

"We need to go faster," said Reagan. "Before we lose the sunlight and can't find our way."

"We have those lamps," I said. "They had lamps in the movie."

Reagan ignored me.

"Let's sing," I said. "To keep our spirits up."

"The hills are alive," sang Reagan, *"with the sound of music."*

I joined in, and we sang our lungs out until we hit the big descent and sped down the icy road, skidding once or twice but never losing control. We went so fast that I got halfway up the next hill by coasting.

Reagan belted out "Climb Every Mountain" as I struggled to pedal us up the hill. Dead Reagan may not have been visible, but deadweight took on a new meaning as I struggled to take us to the top.

"Finally," said Reagan.

"You have no standing to comment," I replied.

This section of Long Road was my favorite. It ran along a section of protected forest and it felt like the middle of a national park.

"I am fourteen going on fifteen," sang Reagan.

"Baby, it's time to think," I yelled.

"I am always fourteen going on fifteen," sang Reagan.

That hit me like a ton of bricks.

"You know how to liven up a party."

"You need to work on your word choice."

I slowed down. Bad idea. We wobbled like the dickens and almost flipped over.

"I have no idea how you kept us on this bike," said Reagan.

"We probably need to head back," I said.

"We can never go back to Austria," said Reagan. "Let's buy some land in the mountains of Vermont that looks like our homeland and start a ski resort."

"Works for me," I said.

I rode us back to the oak tree. We had always stopped there before heading to the real world of Carlow again.

"I wish you could have seen me play yesterday," I said.

"Fourteen points, right?"

"And seven assists. And one rebound by accident."

Reagan laughed. "Amazing. So you can stay on the team as long as you see the shrink?"

"Something like that."

The wind came on stronger, and it blew snow straight at us. I pulled up my jacket collar and wished I had my scarf. And my parka.

"I'm sorry," said Reagan. "For leaving."

The sun disappeared behind a cloud. It grew colder.

"It wasn't your fault," I said. "And I'm the one who left you."

"Would you please let that go?"

I shrugged.

"My heart was one of those things. It was going to be history sooner or later."

"I know," I said.

"I keep thinking about that first Blizzard coach, Coach Taylor? And how he used to say that everyone needed a heart like mine. Boy, was he wrong!"

I shook my head.

"Still," I said. "I should have made you come with me. At least you'd had more time."

"Not much," she said. "It was going to happen. And I'm glad it didn't happen with you there."

"I could have said good-bye," I said.

"No you couldn't," Reagan said. "I was down and dead in a flash."

My eyes welled. "But Andrew shocked your heart into pumping again."

"God, that hurt," she said.

I didn't say anything.

"I was gone, Sam, really gone. That last little blip didn't count for anything." She paused. "That was it. I ended. Reagan Murphy ended."

The finality of it made me gasp.

The breeze knocked the remaining leaf off the oak tree. It

fluttered, like it was a basketball player with great hang time, and then it floated down to the ground to its resting place.

Then Reagan giggled. "I scored on John Rayfield before I went down, though," she said.

"No one told me that!"

"Head-faked the crap out of him!"

"Awesome."

"I'll never forget," said Reagan.

I grinned.

"So," said Reagan.

"So," I replied.

I knew what we needed to do. But I didn't want to be the one to say it.

The wind got stronger.

"So, Sam-I-am," said Reagan. "It's time to say good-bye."

I felt her hand on my shoulder so vividly that I reached up. I swear I felt it.

"It's time," she said.

I knew it was time. It had to be time. But I didn't want it to be time.

"No," I said.

She gripped my shoulder more firmly. "It's time," she said.

I bit my lip to stop the tears from exploding.

I knew that I would always miss Reagan and the missing part would always hurt this bad, but I also knew that I had to say good-bye.

I breathed fast.

"It's okay," she said.

I gripped her hand as hard as I could. I took one long breath to steady myself.

"Good-bye, Reagan," I whispered.

She dug her hand into my shoulder.

"Good-bye, Sam."

And she pulled her hand away and I was alone.

The wind grew so strong that it felt like it was blowing straight through me, like I had no more substance than a ghost. But then the sun poked through a hole in the clouds and lit up the snow around me.

The wind jingled the chains in the outdoor basket.

And I imagined Reagan floating from that basket through that hole and finding her place in the world that lives beyond ours. Maybe it was like our kingdoms down Long Road. Maybe it wasn't like anything I would understand until I got there myself. But for now, I knew I had enough of Reagan left inside me that I would be okay.

I wiped my nose on the back of my gloves and I zipped up as much as I could. And I picked up my bike.

And I headed home.

FILL 'ER UP

One Saturday morning in April, I jogged through Elliot Park. Actually, I ran. I was in such good shape that I ran five miles every morning and did intervals to boot. When I followed the path around the duck pond and headed for the pool, I noticed a white city truck. Two workmen stood inside the pool area, watching water flow from the big spigot at the deep end.

I stopped outside the fence. It was way too early to fill the pool for summer.

"Why are you filling it now?" I asked them.

"We fixed leaks in the pipes," the taller man in overalls said. "And we need to see if it worked."

I nodded, and I watched as they turned the spigot all the way on. Then they locked the gate, climbed into the truck, and drove away.

Water rushed into the pool. It collected at the deep end first, and then it spread until it covered the bottom. The clean water climbing up the freshly painted blue walls was inviting, and I scaled the fence. I sat on the edge of the pool and watched the water rise. The sun warmed my shoulders and neck, and I unzipped my fleece. I lay back on the cement deck and closed my eyes.

Birds chirped in the nearby trees and some toddler yelled, "Higher, higher," to the babysitter pushing her swing. A light breeze rustled the edges of my running shorts and the sun felt great on my face.

I was so relaxed that I nodded off.

Yelling kids woke me up. A pack of boys skidded around the corner on their bikes, the two in the lead carrying basket-balls. They pedaled to the outdoor court and tossed their bikes on the ground. Within minutes, they were caught up in a pickup game. The air filled with the sounds of dribbling, trash talking, shots banging the backboard, shots clanging the rims, and shots jangling the metal nets.

I closed my eyes again and listened to the rushing water, the birds, the shrieking toddlers, and the basketball game. I wanted to swim, I wanted to swing, I wanted to play ball.

I stood and pulled myself back over the fence. After watching the pool fill for a few more minutes, I resumed my run, heading to the sledding hill with an easy gait.

When I started to climb, the half hearts clanged against my chest. I smiled, thinking of Reagan.

Then I sprinted to the top, swinging my muscled arms hard until I reached the top. I stopped on High Street and stood tall, proud that I was barely winded.

Sam-I-am. Dribble Queen strong.

ACKNOWLEDGMENTS

I would like to thank my writing comrades, Debby Dahl Edwardson, Jane Buchanan, and Sarah Sullivan, for their ready insights and constant encouragement. Thanks also to the community that is Vermont College of Fine Arts for providing such a rich and supportive environment for me. I have lasting memories of lectures, workshops, readings, discussions, laughs, and more.

A big dose of gratitude goes to my agent, Melissa Nasson, who, along with Rubin Pfeffer, believed in this story from its very beginnings. Thanks to Stephen Roxburgh for his feedback and the questions that shaped its final form. Special thanks to publisher Sonali Fry for choosing it as part of the launch of Bonnier Publishing USA's newest imprint, Yellow Jacket.

Finally, a big thanks to Kim Bailey for her support and patience as I pursue writing in a dual-career life.